CLOSE-UP

ALSO BY SHERRY ASHWORTH

Paralysed

Winner of the South Lanarkshire
Children's Book of the Year

Also shortlisted for:

The Red House Children's Book Award
The Redbridge Children's Book Award
The Leicester Children's Book of the Year

SHERRY ASHWORTH
CLOSE-UP

SIMON AND SCHUSTER

Thanks to team Ashworth - Brian,
Robyn and Rachel; Stephen Cole;
Peter Marsden at Starbucks

SIMON AND SCHUSTER
First published in Great Britain by Simon & Schuster UK Ltd, 2006
Africa House, 64-78 Kingsway, London WC2B 6AH
A CBS COMPANY

Simon & Schuster UK Ltd
Africa House, 64–78 Kingsway,
London WC2B 6AH.

A CIP catalogue record for this book is available from the British Library

ISBN 1 416 90474 3
EAN 9781416 904748

1 3 5 7 9 10 8 6 4 2

Typeset by Rowland Phototypesetting Ltd, Bury St Edmunds, Suffolk
Printed and bound in Great Britain by Cox & Wyman Ltd, Reading, Berks

www.simonsays.co.uk

For Paul

Dusk falls late in summer, and the man waits until it is dusk before he saunters up the leafy street. His eyes scan the grey wheelie bins left outside the houses, reading the numbers painted on them. 28. 30. 32.

He stops now and looks about him. No one around. Good. He positions himself between the bin and the over-grown hedge shielding the front garden of number 32. He pauses, then sidles along until he reaches a point where his body is obscured, but he can see the door with its coloured glass panels and the sitting room, where the curtains have not yet been drawn.

Motionless, hardly breathing, the beat of his blood almost audible in his ears, he watches.

He watches the woman searching some shelves, partly obscured from his view. She's dressed in jeans and a cream-coloured fleece. His eyes flick past her to the brown corduroy settee where a young man is slumped, his legs sprawling, his eyes fixed on a TV screen.

'Jimmy,' he mutters. '*My* Jimmy.'

'Jimmy? I can't find the *Psycho* DVD – the one I bought last weekend.'

1

My mum's head's cocked on one side as she reads the sides of the DVD cases.

'Jimmy? Are you sure you haven't borrowed it?'

I think for a moment. I did watch it a few days ago – but not upstairs in my room – I was round at Chris's – did I bring it home? Don't remember. I shift about on the settee, pick up the remote and channel-hop a bit.

'Stop that,' says Mum. 'You're annoying me. Well?'

I fling down the remote. 'Dunno. I did watch it last week,' I concede.

If this was a movie, there'd be background music now, a few slow, deep notes building in speed as my mum straightens, turns, and looks at me.

'So where is it?'

'I'll have a look in my room later.'

'Jimmy – I want to watch it *now*!'

I'm quickly rewinding in my mind to when I was at Chris's place on Monday. After the film we had a few cans of beer, then I headed out empty-handed. I remember getting my bus ticket out to show the driver and thinking, I've left the DVD at Chris's place. But, hey, it isn't as if it's a big deal. I can get it back in a few days.

'I think I might have left it at Chris's,' I say.

The background music reaches a crescendo and explodes. There's a steady jungle-style drumbeat. Well, there isn't really, but you follow my meaning. My mum turns on me.

'I haven't even bloody *seen* it yet! You've got no right to nick things I've bought and take them round your friends.'

'Hey, chill,' I tell her. 'I'll get it back. I'll call round tomorrow.' Then I remember. Chris is on holiday. He went with his family to Florida and he's there for a fortnight. This is not good.

'Maybe not tomorrow,' I add hastily. ''Cause I'm working all day at Coffee Corp.'

There's this mythical creature – the basilisk – if it eyes you, you turn to stone. That was the look my mum gave me. I'm trying to work out how to get from the settee to the door without crossing her path.

'You don't give a damn about anyone else, Jimmy. And especially you don't give a damn about ME!'

'Not true!' I shout, as I scramble off the settee, make for the door and take the stairs two at a time, run along the landing, and up again until I reach my bedroom.

And it isn't true. I love my mum, really. It's just that . . . how can I put this . . . she's got it in for me.

I know what you're thinking. That arguing about a DVD is pretty pathetic. You can get old movies like *Psycho* dead cheap these days. I know I've made my mum sound mean and uptight but she isn't all the time. She was then, though. We have over fifty DVDs in our house. What's so special about *Psycho*? Well, admittedly it's arguably Hitchcock's finest work, excepting *The Birds*, and the shower sequence with Janet Leigh is one of my five top horror moments of all time but, hey, I'm digressing. You want the lowdown on me and my mum, Carol.

But let me set the scene first. You've already got the voice-over – this is me, talking. It's my voice you're hearing. So now – as well as listening to me – picture me in my room now –

I've got the attic bedroom. Imagine a camera positioned in the doorway, panning around. There's a tiny window, a navy blue square, as it's getting dark now. Next turn and focus on a wardrobe with the door open, and my gear spilling out of it – wardrobe not big enough. A TV/DVD combi on a chest of drawers, of which none shut properly – too much stuff. And an ummade bed snug under the sloping roof, with that black and white poster of James Dean stuck on it, except one corner has come loose of its Blu-tack and hangs down vertically. I reach up (because I'm on the bed) and try and fail to stick it back on.

That tells you everything you need to know, as you can read cinematic images. The attic bedroom – that sets me apart from my family (Mum, Steve my step-dad, and the kids Stacey and Kyle). I'm like the Outsider, the one that doesn't fit. Yeah, that's cool. *The Outsider*. A film noir starring Colin Farrell as me. Once Melanie at school said I looked a bit like Colin Farrell, which was a chat-up line if ever you heard one, you will agree. Then all the mess – that tells you I'm a tortured genius, in the process of finding himself (and a clean pair of socks – I keep forgetting to put them in the wash). And the James Dean poster – that I'm young and cool and angry. And also that movies are my life, and one day I'm going to be a movie director. I'm serious. Completely and absolutely serious. I bought that TV/DVD combi myself – with the money Gran left, though it didn't stretch to a camcorder, worst luck. *Gran* always believed in me. In her memory I watch as many movies as I can. So how can my mum say I lack ambition? The fact I put in no work for my

AS Levels is because strictly they're not relevant. And anyway, like shooting a movie, you can always retake. Right now, I'm more into developing my own vision, my own signature. I don't want to be like anyone else, I'm not Tarantino or Hitchcock or Spielberg or the Coen brothers, especially as there are two of them. I'm me, whoever he is.

Good line, that. 'I'm me, whoever he is.' Yeah. Like it.

So I lie there, smiling, I've forgotten about the spat with my mum, and the only cloud in my mind is that fact that I've got to get up at five fifteen tomorrow morning. Yeah, you heard me right. Five fifteen. I'm on the early shift at Coffee Corp, where I serve the coolest cappuccinos in town. Oh yeah, I said I'd tell you about me and my mum. But you don't really want to know. There's not much to say. Mums aren't interesting, they're just *there*. Like the walls of your house – boring but necessary. And you ignore them until they start looking for the *Psycho* DVD you borrowed, know what I'm saying?

But when I accept my first Oscar, it'll all be different. 'The one person I want to thank, the one person who made it possible for me to be here today, in every sense of the word – the most important lady in my life, my inspiration – let's hear it for Carol Keane!' The spotlight finds her out and a diamond tear glistens on her cheek. She's so proud of me she can hardly speak.

I could give you the rest of my acceptance speech – I work on it most nights. In fact, as I wriggle out of my jeans and lean right out of bed to switch the telly on, I think I might adjust it slightly as I drop off to sleep – I could insert a joke about the *Psycho* DVD, so my mum remembers the bad old days and smiles through her tears. Nice one!

I'm smiling to myself as I settle down for an early night.

LIZ'S DIARY

Thursday 26th July

First entry

I am starting a diary:

Because I'm bored. Because I haven't written a diary since I was fourteen. But mainly because I came up to bed early as I have to wake at five tomorrow for the early shift at Coffee Corp. I couldn't sleep, so I decided to tidy my desk, and found this notebook that I'm writing in now. It's got a greeny-brown marbled cover with an olive binding and is dead old-fashioned. Someone must have given it to me as a present, but I can't think who.

I opened the first page and when I saw its creamy blankness I itched to make my mark. I love writing – not just the feel of the pen pressing ever so gently but relentlessly on the page, but also making things real. When you put things into words, they stay for ever.

But I don't want to write stories. I have no time for those. Like, what's the point of making stuff up when this whole crazy world is waiting to be understood and worked out and made sense of. Writing stories is like lying, in a way. Pure fiction. So that's why I'm writing a diary – everything you're about to read in here is true. I won't exaggerate or varnish or hide anything, even if it's painful and embarrassing. So, Maggie, if you're reading this (she won't be – but mums have a habit of accidentally picking up your diary!) don't say you haven't been warned.

So – for posterity – I'm Elizabeth Burns, seventeen, and I live with my mum, Maggie. People call me Liz. Those are the bare facts. What am I like? Ordinary. Well, no. No one likes to think they're just ordinary. I'm not one of those pink, fluffy, girlie girls – there are so many of them at college like with their straightened hair and low-cut trousers. I'm not a Goth, though I can see where they're coming from. My hair's short, and gelled into spikes when I can be bothered. I had red bits put in a few months ago and they're still visible. I haven't got ready for bed yet, so I'm still in my Che Guevara T-shirt and brown combats. Lookswise, my eyes are too large and my nose too small. I wear a nose-ring. I've thought about getting other piercings but I'm not sure.

Other stuff about me – I'm currently single. I have had a couple of boyfriends but both were disasters. The first one was when I was only fourteen and I wanted to see what it was like, going out with someone. It lasted a month until he proposed marriage – at fourteen! That gave me second thoughts. So I finished with him. Last year I went out with Darren because I thought he was cool. He always so looked so miserable and I thought I could cheer him up. He was brooding and discontented and sold the *Socialist Worker* in the city over the road from McDonald's. Only he turned out to be a) boring, b) more cheered up by the weed he smoked than me, and then he was even more boring, and c) dying to get me into bed which was even more boring still. So I finished with him too.

Now I'm perfectly happy not having a boyfriend, despite the fact that all the girls at college are boy-obsessed. I mean, it's sad. Here we are in the twenty-first century and still girls are rating themselves by whether boys fancy them or not, or thinking having a boyfriend makes you whole in some weird way. What I'm saying is that I don't want a relationship – they always end in tears. Just getting off with blokes is OK, having fun, having a laugh. But as soon as you start trusting someone or depending on someone, you risk being let down.

If I'm being really honest – and that's the purpose of this diary – I know I think this way because of what happened to Maggie and my dad. She's told me all about it. When I was a baby she discovered that all the time she'd been pregnant with me, he'd been having an affair. Listen to this – when she went into labour and she rang him at work, he wasn't there, and his mates tried to cover up for him, but he was with that woman. So everything was pretty awful after I was born.

Maggie kicked Dad out and I grew up not knowing him at all. He married the woman he was having that affair with and on their wedding day Maggie threw a party. All her mates came round and they got wasted. Mum ended up on the table doing a Shirley Bassey imitation. How cool is that? My dad lives abroad now and he writes to me at Christmas and on my birthday. Weird, but I'm used to it. I don't need him, anyhow.

Maggie's a probation officer and good at her job. We're more like best mates than mum and daughter, and I like it like that. There isn't anything I couldn't tell her. There isn't anything she wouldn't tell me. Like tonight, she's at a party. Cerys, her mate from the local Amnesty group, is having a do as she's turned forty. Maggie borrowed my leather boots which she teamed up with a long black skirt and black bodice top. She looked ace. Peter's going to be there – Peter is this bloke she sees occasionally – her boyfriend, sort of. But with him being a journalist, he's often not here for days on end. So he's a part-time boyfriend, which suits her. She's arranged to get a taxi home as she reckons there's going to be plenty to drink. She said not to wait up for her but it's weird – I can't go to sleep unless I know she's in the house. I don't exactly worry about her but I like to know she's safe. She does the same for me.

So that's me – and my mum – and this is my diary. Already three pages are full with black looping words. My handwriting's messy but that's because I spend more time typing on the keyboard on my computer. Writing like this feels old-fashioned, but more real, more direct. I want to carry on but I'm running out of things to say.

More facts. I'm studying Psychology, History, English and Politics and I'll be getting my AS results mid-August. Meantime I'm working at Coffee Corp in the city. I got the job back in February when it was just about the only opportunity available. Even though I could get something better now, I'll stick with it as I know the routine and the manager, Bob, is pretty decent. The rest of the staff are OK – Charlene is cool and so is Amir. But because we all have different shifts you never know who you're going to be working with.

There's a chance that tomorrow I might end up working with Jimmy.

Jimmy. I've been putting off writing about him. Sometimes he drives me mad – he's a walking disaster. It's like he lives on a different planet to the rest of us, daydreaming, bumping into things – but Bob reckons he's good with the punters so he keeps him on. But that's not the whole truth. Sometimes I watch him working and I know I've been watching him too long, so I have to wrest my eyes away. Or if he smiles at me, I feel myself blush. Can you fancy a boy when you haven't given yourself permission to fancy him? Because this is what I do know – you should NEVER have relationships with people at work, and also that Jimmy and I don't have anything in common, and like I said before, I don't WANT a boyfriend – because they're always bad news – and so I keep my feelings about Jimmy strictly to myself. And these feelings are purely academic, because he doesn't know I exist. Well, of course he does know I exist, because we work together, but he hasn't noticed me. Not as a girl. Which is just as well. And I'm going to keep it that way.

My God – it's already half eleven. I should be in bed. Shall I text Maggie and see if she's on her way home? I might – if she doesn't come back in half an hour.

I will text her now – it's past midnight.

I've done it.

I'm waiting – I'm in my large Homer Simpson T-shirt which I wear for bed. I've set the alarm and I'm wondering how on earth I'll get up in the morning. I'm writing this in bed, the book propped on my knees.

Ah – a message.

Peter's bringing her home – she's not taking a taxi. Says she'll be home in fifteen.

Well, I hope he's not been drinking.

JIMMY

The alarm explodes, my hand crashes down on it and it dawns on me this isn't a joke – I really have to get up at five fifteen a.m. I roll out of bed and into my clothes, stumble to the bathroom and catch a glimpse of my face in the mirror. Hello, zombie! Just like *The Night of the Living Dead*. I stagger around the bathroom doing that living dead walk, hands out in front of me, glassy-eyed face, and it makes me smile and wakes me up.

When I get out onto the still-dark street, I realise I'm wide awake, but the rest of the world isn't. The sky's almost black and the houses as still as the stones they're made of. It's chilly, even though it's summer. I wriggle into my jacket as I walk along the street. My footsteps echo. It's a ten-minute walk to the train. I plug some music in my ears for the soundtrack.

Hey, I'm liking this. Liking being completely alone in the darkened street and knowing everyone else is fast asleep and dreaming, spinning their own crazy stories. The road's completely deserted, like after a natural disaster. Because if you were making a disaster movie you could start right here, a street where people live where there's nobody – all human life has vanished. Only a solitary figure (me) looking for signs that just one other person (female, preferably) has survived the catastrophe.

Then I'm in the main road and in front of me is the train station where a man's raising the iron grille so the first passengers can get down to the platform. I buy my ticket and as I descend to the platform I notice I'm not alone. There's a bloke in a donkey jacket and someone else of my age. Then another bloke comes down the steps, anxiously scanning the platform. He's well dressed but dishevelled. We're all locked into our own private worlds. The headlight of the train approaches. I push the panel that opens the doors, and take a window seat. The carriage shudders and clunks forward, and the train rattles away, gathering speed.

Outside the navy sky has got richer – not light yet – but there's a hidden radiance, almost gold – like someone had thrown blue silk over a block of raw gold. I'm high up and the camera in my head is looking down over the houses – they're coal-black and their windows blacker still, except here and there I see squares of light where one or two people are early risers like me. So, OK, I focus on them to see if anyone's standing there completely starkers – it does happen. But mainly I'm looking at the changing colour of the sky as it brightens, and I don't only see it but feel it tingling in my veins.

The city comes towards us, tower blocks of patchwork lights, and it swallows us up whole. When I get out at the main station with the other passengers I see a couple on a bench still dressed up from the night before. Their late night and my early morning have got tangled up and inseparable.

We grin at each other, kind of acknowledging the fact.

I check my watch and I'm going to be on time. I'm feeling good, and walk quickly to Coffee Corp humming a tune.

I'm prepping the crème base for the happy frappé machine, when Liz walks in. She's bleary-eyed and her hair's sticking up all over the place. She looks like she's just got out of bed.

'Morning!' I grin at her. 'Aren't you glad to be alive?'

'Sorry I'm late.' She ignores me and addresses her comment to Bob who's checking and issuing our floats for the till. 'I overslept. My mum got in late and it woke me up. I didn't get to sleep properly till two a.m.'

'Your mum a bit of a raver, then?' I joke.

'Oh, sod off, Jimmy.'

I shrug. Liz and a sense of humour are as far apart as the Arctic and the Antarctic. Did you know you only get penguins at one pole – either the Arctic or the Antarctic? But which one?

'Which pole do you get penguins at?' I ask.

Bob and Liz stare at me.

'The north or south pole?'

'The south pole,' Liz spits. 'Which is where I wish you were now.'

'Welcome to Coffee Corp,' Bob says. 'The friendly stop for your early-morning coffee. Where the staff love being here and love each other.'

'Sod off,' we both say to him.

*

You must have been inside a Coffee Corp, so I don't need to describe it much. There's the counter with the glass cabinet of panini sandwiches waiting to be grilled, cookies and muffins; the bar where we make the coffee, the till, the serving point, all along a curved counter, cutting us off from the café proper, with its *Friends*-style comfy chairs and low tables, bar stools at the window where busy punters can sip their espressos while looking out on the street, block images on the walls of swirling cityscapes and in the background some easy-listening track, Sinatra or Dean Martin. It's cool. I like it here. I can imagine I'm in Manhattan, and Ross and Rachel might walk in anytime.

But this morning I'm standing by the sink watching the punters and it reminds me of the opening sequence of *Pulp Fiction*. It's the way they're all sitting there so unsuspecting – the mum with her two kids in the corner who are colouring in Coffee Corp posters, the man reading *The Times* by the window with his PDA by his side, the woman looking at the stand of Coffee Corp mugs. Because if that couple at the far table jumped up and now and the woman said – how does it go? – 'Everybody be cool – this is a robbery . . . Don't move or I'll execute every last—'

'Jimmy! There's a queue and you're on the till!'

Shit. There is and I am.

'Thanks, Liz,' I say and I hear her sigh loudly. That girl has got in for me.

'Umm . . . a latte . . . make that a skinny latte – no – just a latte – regular – no – grande umm . . .'

'Take away or stay here?' I ask the punter.

16

'Umm ... take out – no – stay in.' Hmm. I like the decisive types.

'Grande latte,' I shout to Liz, who's on the bar. My accent's fake Italian. I mark the drinks ID note and stick it on the ceramic mug with its brown lettering – *Coffee Corp*. I grin at the middle-aged lady who's ordered the coffee. 'It will be ready pronto,' I say. 'Over at the serving point. And enjoy!' I wink at her. Heck, she's old enough to be my mother but right now I'm John Travolta – this is how he would serve coffee. I ring her order on the till and take her money.

Next one in the queue – middle-aged bloke, in a blue shirt, casual jacket over his arm, high-waisted trousers. His cheeks are jowly, sagging a little. There's a splash of feathery scars like splinters across one side of his face and his fore-head. His eyes fix on mine almost as if he's going to ask me something more important than the request that stumbles from his lips.

'Just a coffee.'

He sounds embarrassed – has this guy been in a Coffee Corp before? Maybe he's an ex-con, just released from jail.

'OK,' I say, patient. 'You mean a filter coffee? Or an Americano with milk?'

'That will do,' he says.

'An Americano?'

He nods.

'Regular? Grande? Maxi?'

'Maxi.'

'One Maxi Americano,' I call to Liz. For some reason I don't joke. This geezer has given me the creeps. He's still standing in front of me, and I don't like the way he's staring.

'The serving point's to your right,' I say, polite. 'If you wait there your coffee will arrive.'

And then he smiles at me, as if he's just recognised me, as if he was on the verge of saying something significant. I'm spooked. But he moves away, and I'm aware the queue's grown even longer and Bob has come out the back. Time to look sharp.

Twenty minutes later, Charlene comes in from her break and Bob says she can have a spin on the till while I clear some tables. I get the multi-purpose spray disinfectant and some paper towel and go out into the café. That bloke's still there – his coffee is long finished and he's not reading the paper folded on the table in front of him. He's looking at me. I kind of grin.

Then I think this is just like a spy movie. The creepy bloke could have mistaken me for his contact, and he's waiting for me to give the password – but he's confident I know it so he sits there just waiting. And when I do he passes me a microchip that I insert in my computer and discover the secret weaponry of the country that's planning to take over the civilised world. A bit like Tom Cruise in *Mission Impossible*. And I'm deep into this and thinking whether I want a chronological narrative or to mess around with the time frame when someone says, 'Excuse me.'

I look up, and fall in love.

She's tall, even a bit taller than me, in a tiny white T-shirt, low jeans with a wide, studded belt, and her long hair is braided and decorated with beads. Her skin's tanned and her teeth gleam.

'Yeah?' I say. I'm lost, I'm drowning.

'Does Liz Burns work here?'

'Liz who?' I say, playing for time.

'Liz Bu— oh – Liz! Liz!!' she squeals, and wriggles with delight. She runs over to her and I can't catch what they're talking about. As I move from table to table, removing empties, squirting cleaning fluid, I keep an eye on that babe. I notice Bob's been called over and is introduced. Next thing, she's coming back into the café clutching a Coffee Corp application form. She sits down by the window, takes a pen from her shoulder bag, and starts filling it in.

I sidle up to Liz.

'Who's she?'

'Sophie – someone I know from college.'

'Is she looking for a job here?'

'Yeah.' Then she changes the subject. 'Do you know that bloke sitting in the corner?'

'Nope.'

'He's watching us.'

'Some freak, I guess. Tell me about Sophie.'

Liz eyes me in that way she has, like she's looking straight through you. 'Like, whether she has a boyfriend or not?'

'That's not a bad place to begin.'

'Double espresso and iced tea!' calls Charlene.

Liz turns to make the drinks.

I feel a bit bad. Should you let one girl know you fancy another? I think maybe I've hurt Liz's feelings. Even though she's not my type, she is kind of sexy – no, not sexy – what am I saying here? But you could see how blokes would find her attractive. If they liked being bossed around. So I decide to try to make amends. I move up to her and put an arm round her waist.

'You know, I've never asked – have *you* got a boyfriend?'

'I'm married,' she says. 'To a Sumo wrestler. And when I tell him you've been sexually harassing me he's going to come here and sit on your face.'

'All right, already!' I joke.

I turn around and there's Sophie with her completed form. Her handwriting's large and she dots her 'i's with hearts. Kinda cute. She hands me her form and as she moves towards me I can smell her perfume – fresh and expensive.

'I'll give this to Bob,' I say, and find my mouth's stuck in a grin. I can't unfreeze it. She gives a tinkly kind of laugh – she's the Keira Knightley type. A girl like that – you could do anything with her. No – not in that way – but you could cast her in a romcom, a historical epic, a sci-fi thriller – in a tight metallic spacesuit showing every curve. I'm still grinning. This is ridiculous.

Bob intervenes. 'That's for me, thank you,' he says. 'I believe it's time for the toilets to be cleaned,' he tells me.

I actually feel myself blushing – can you believe it? So I duck and run. I get the cleaning stuff I need and enter the toilet.

This is not my favourite job. But I cope by thinking about other things. I decide to work out my finances. I get paid tomorrow. That means I can pay off a few of my debts. Can

I afford to buy my mum another copy of *Psycho*? Or ought I to pay back Amir the twenty quid I borrowed off him in the week? Or just blow the whole lot on taking Sophie out for dinner?

I think about the toilet from hell in *Trainspotting*, the one Ewan McGregor falls into, and I tell myself the bog in Coffee Corp in Cross Street isn't that bad. Then I'm getting ready to spray the sink and give it a quick wipe, when I notice something in it. A stick-thing with a blue line on it – I know what that is – a pregnancy test. I am completely grossed out, but luckily I'm wearing plastic gloves so I pick it up gingerly and toss it into the black rubbish bag I've got with me. And it's at exactly that moment my mobile vibrates in my pocket. I stop what I'm doing to pick up. Cool. Amir. It's his day off today.

He's asking if I fancy a curry tonight then maybe a film later with some of his mates. Yeah, sure, I say, I'm not doing anything. Yeah, eight o'clock – which'll give me time to get home, rested and out again. I have a slight pang of regret just in case Sophie's hanging around outside the bog. But, heck, she'll have to wait for me. I mustn't give her the impression I'm up for grabs.

In a few moments I'm finished and as I come out there's that bloke again, waiting to go in. He looks startled as we collide, and backs off. This time I don't get that creepy feeling. Or it's more like I've known him for ages. Weird. Anyway, I look around for Sophie but there's no sign. Liz is back of house when I go to put the cleaning stuff away and I'm about to ask her more about Sophie but there's something about her that puts me off. She's sitting by the table lost in thought. I get the read-out that something's wrong. I'm not even sure she's noticed I'm there.

Immediately I get the picture – that pregnancy test – it was Liz's! Bloody hell! Poor kid – putting a brave face on it, but all the time worrying she's knocked up. I decide on the spot that I'll be there for her. I cough slightly to alert her to my presence. The camera would zoom into me then, close up on my concerned expression.

'Liz,' I say. 'It's OK. I know.'

She swivels round. 'What? Know what?'

'I found the pregnancy test,' I tell her.

'The pregnancy test?'

'Yeah – the one you left – in – the . . .'

Her face changes from blank incomprehension through dawning realisation to utter amazement. For the first time it strikes me Liz ought to have a screen test. She has potential.

'You found a pregnancy test and thought I was pregnant!'

Now she starts laughing. I kind of grin – I've never seen her laugh like that before. It's infectious and I join in. There are even tears in her eyes.

Eventually she subsides and says, 'Thanks, Jimmy. I needed that.' Then, 'How dare you think that a) I'm such an idiot I'd get myself accidentally pregnant and b) that I would do something so minging as leave the test in the loo. Now shove off – it's my break and I want to be alone!'

I want to be alone. Now who said that? Some old movie star – one of those blonde vamps with platinum hair and sultry eyes. Mae West? No – she said, come up and see me sometime. Marilyn Monroe? No. I've got it – Greta Garbo. It was old Garbo. *I vant to be alone* – in a German accent.

I vant to be alone. I mug the line as I return to front of house.

'Bob,' I say. 'I vant to be alone!'

LIZ'S DIARY

Friday 27th July

Second entry

When I started this yesterday I was just messing. I was writing for the sake of it. But now I really do have something to write about. And I'm glad I have this book because I can work out what's happening and what I think about it.

It started late last night, when I was waiting for Maggie. I was lying on my back in bed with my eyes closed, knowing I should fall asleep, but unable to do so as my senses were alert. Eventually I heard a car coast along our street and come to a halt. I waited to hear Mum's key in the lock but there was nothing, so I thought this couldn't be her and Peter. I sat up in bed and knelt so I could move the curtain to one side and see down into the road. Peter's car still had its headlights on. It had pulled up right outside our house. I watched.

Peter got out of the driver's seat, came round, and opened the passenger door. Maggie got out. Then he caught her in his arms and they kissed. I was taken aback and immediately I closed the curtain, my heart thudding.

I was taken aback because I wasn't expecting it – and also that I'd put myself in the position of a snooper, looking out of the window like that, seeing my mum being kissed. It was wrong of me. But I was also surprised because now that I think of it, I've never, ever seen my mum kiss Peter before. I mean, why should I? I know she goes out with him from time to time, but that's a part of her life she keeps on one side. Seeing Peter kiss her then made the whole thing real for me – and more than that, it hit me that while I'd been involved with my exams, they might have been getting closer. And I hadn't realised. I could tell all that just by the way they kissed – like there was no one else in the world for either of them.

That's why I didn't get to sleep for ages. My light was off so it was easy for me to pretend to be asleep. I listened carefully just in case she'd brought Peter in with her, but I knew she wouldn't do that really. That was one of our unwritten rules. He doesn't stay over. He didn't stay over last night. Instead, all I heard were my mum's bedtime noises – muffled, so as not to wake me. Then all was still. I needed to sleep. I had to be to be up at five for work.

I only had three and a half hours' kip. So all day I felt as if I was only half alive. The stuff with Maggie was at the back of my mind, but I can't say I was obsessed or anything. I had to use all the concentration I had to get the orders right at work.

Oh, and Sophie came in to apply for a job. I don't know how I feel about that. It's not that we don't get on – we do. She's not one of my mates, but in class she'll sit next to me if there's a space, and act as if she's pleased to be with me. She's always friendly and yet ... hmm ... she's the kind of girl who makes you feel inferior. Is it because she's good-looking? I wouldn't like to think so, because if it was, then it's my fault for being envious. But Charlene is good-looking – think Beyoncé and you're almost there – and she doesn't make me feel like that. No, Sophie has a subtle way of making me feel bad about myself. But I can't put my finger on why. I don't relish the prospect of working with her.

And then Jimmy's eyes were out on stalks! I mean, how embarrassing! You could see Sophie really playing up to him. If I have to witness the two of them all over each other! But I'm not going to imagine the worst – the chances are that they'll deploy her at another branch. Then, while she was filling out her application form, he put his arm round my waist while I was at the bar. I wasn't expecting it. And he asked me if I had a boyfriend. Luckily I can be pretty quick when it comes to repartee. Then afterwards, for ages, it was like my body could remember the pressure of his arm around my waist – tight and snug.

Jimmy can be alternately lovely and infuriating. And thick. When I was on my break and thinking about Maggie, he came in and actually thought some pregnancy test he'd cleared was mine! It makes me wonder how he sees me, and how little he knows about me. But whose fault is that?

But when I left Coffee Corp at two, something strange happened. That man, the one who'd been hanging around all morning staring at Jimmy, he was still there. That's not entirely unusual. We get all sorts at Coffee Corp – drop-outs with just enough cash for one coffee, who sit nursing their drink all day. Bob says to leave them to it if they're not bothering anyone. But this bloke didn't look poor and was dressed quite normally. It was the way he was watching Jimmy that made me pay attention. Then, on my way out, he spoke to me.

'Are you a friend of Jimmy's?' he asked.

'I work with him,' I said. I wanted to get away but the bloke stood in front of me. The pavement was busy with tourists, shoppers and city types.

'How is he?' he said. 'What's he doing now?'

'Sorry,' I said. 'I don't know.' A bit scared without knowing why, I left him.

That *was* weird, no? I was halfway to the bus stop before I thought I should have gone back to Coffee Corp to warn Jimmy. I would have texted him, but I don't have his number. Next time I see him, though, I'll certainly say something.

I went home, made some tea, and went straight to bed. When I woke up it was six in the evening. I lay on my bed for a bit, trying to pick up the pieces of the day. Once I'd got my head together, I made my way downstairs and there was Maggie, preparing a salad.

'Good time last night?' I asked her, yawning.

'Yeah,' she said. 'It was fun.'

Was that all she was telling me? I sensed instinctively she was holding something back. Maggie and I are so close that we can pick up on how each other is feeling.

'You were home late,' I said.

'I know. I hope you didn't wait up.'

'I was in bed,' I told her, which was the truth.

I watched her for a bit. Our kitchen is one of those long, narrow ones they call a galley kitchen, like on a boat. The sink's in the middle along one side and the window looks out onto the yard. Mum had put the chopping board near the sink so she could wash and prepare the vegetables. Her fingers were practised and confident. I was mesmerised by their deft movements. But I found I couldn't look at her face. Maggie's hair is short and neat, and she won't be seen dead without her mascara. She generally wears trousers – combats – and today she wore a grey shirt on top. People say we resemble each other. I can't see it, myself. She lifted a glistening, damp carrot and pressed it against the grater. I watched the carrot get smaller and smaller.

'Liz,' Maggie said. 'I want to talk to you about something.'

'Yeah?'

'About Peter.'

'OK.' I felt myself tense.

'The lease has come up for renewal on his flat. And he's in a bit of a quandary, because the situation at the *Courier* office isn't stable. As you know.'

I did know. The *Courier*'s a national newspaper, and Peter was sent here to run a newsdesk for our area. That was about six months ago, and that was when Maggie first met him. But apparently the deputy editor of the sister local newspaper was furious his girlfriend didn't get the job, and has been stirring it for Peter, saying he's incompetent. Which according to Maggie is bollocks, as Peter is a great reporter. But the worst-case scenario is that Vince, this deputy editor, gets Peter sent back to London. That's what Maggie meant, about the situation not being stable.

'So rather than take out a new lease, we were wondering . . . I was wondering . . . if Peter might bed down here for a while.'

That jolted me. I wasn't prepared. I was stiff and awkward as I responded to her.

'But we only have two bedrooms,' I stumbled.

Maggie was just silent. Then I felt a surge of anger. Because what was really going on here was that she wanted him to move in with us. And she'd never hinted to me this was a possibility. Had it not been for the glimpse that I got of them last night, I'd have just imagined the whole relationship was casual. But it wasn't. And I'd been left in the dark.

'I don't know,' I said.

'Think about it,' Maggie replied, and picked up another carrot.

I thought, two's company, but three's a crowd.

Like I've said, with there just being the two of us, Maggie and I had become best mates. She was my mum, older sister, best friend, confidante all rolled into one. My friends have always been jealous of me and with reason. Their parents give them hell sometimes, they're unreasonable, or too shockable, or too distant – but I have the perfect mother. We do – did – everything together. Until now.

Standing there, I knew I had a choice. I could wander into the living room and put on the TV, and just blank all this out. Or I could face her now and tell her what was really on my mind. I chose the latter.

'Look – this isn't about his lease, is it? You're really into him, and you haven't let me know. And now you want to move in together.'

Maggie froze and I knew I'd scored bulls-eye. After a long moment, she turned to face me.

'I'm sorry,' she said. 'There's some truth in that. In the beginning it really was only a casual thing – I could never imagine myself falling seriously for someone again. Then, when I realised we were getting more involved, I got nervous. I was shy of telling you. I kept putting it off. I didn't know how you'd react.'

This hurt me even more. She hadn't only kept her feelings secret from me, but actually thought that if she did, I'd throw a hissy fit. What did she take me for? Some kind of spoiled brat? I was upset, but not because of Peter, but because she didn't trust me, because I thought we were closer than *she* seemed to think, because . . . it was all a stupid mess.

Through gritted teeth I said, 'I am grown up, you know. You could have said something.'

Then she beamed at me. This was the permission she'd been craving.

'He's lovely, Liz. I haven't felt like this before, ever. He's kind, he's intelligent, he's principled – and the chemistry is right. When we're together, it's . . .'

Stop! – too much information, I'm thinking to myself.

'And I just know you'll like him as much as I do.'

I hope not! I added silently.

'Now listen – I don't want you to think for one moment

this will affect you or our relationship. You know how much I love you, and that you'll always come first.'

'Mum – it's fine,' I said.

'Come here!' She hugged me tight and I hugged her back.

'I'm happy for you,' I muttered.

'So will you think about what I said?'

'Yeah.'

And the evening went on and we watched TV and eventually turned in, and here I am sitting by my desk again writing this. I think I said all the right things to Maggie. I don't think I've spoiled it for her. I want her to have a good time with this Peter. I can see, looking into the future, that once I go to uni, she'll be alone and in need of company. So honestly I don't mind one bit. I don't mind that she's falling in love.

But I don't see why he should have to come and live here.

I don't want to have him there when me and Maggie are just chilling. I don't want to have to hide my head in the pillow when I know they're in bed together. I don't want to have to think of them kissing in the way they did the other night. I don't want him interfering in my life. I don't even know him! I've met him a few times – on his way in or out. He's just a stranger. How can she expect me to just say yeah, right, bring him in. She hasn't even given me a chance to get to know him.

The truth is, I feel upset, betrayed and scared. I also feel a right cow for feeling this way. That's why I've decided I'm going to have to lighten up. I mean, there is a funny side. My mum is having a better love life than me!

I've got to stop myself slipping into a self-pitying black hole. I have a tendency to be moody – it's one of my weaknesses. But it's not like I decide to have a mood – one just wells up and takes me over.

Only this time I won't let it. I'm going to cheer myself up. I'm going to damn well have as much fun as Maggie is having.

OK, diary, I am going out tomorrow night. Wherever. With whoever. And I'm going to make absolutely sure I enjoy myself. To the limit.

JIMMY

I get back from work on Friday completely and utterly knackered. But the house is empty so I fall asleep on the settee for an hour or so until Stacey and Kyle get in from school. They stay on in Late Club so Mum can pick them up. Though she runs her beauty business from home, she's booked up most of the time and out on the road. Kyle bounds in and jumps on me so we mock-wrestle for a bit, then Mum comes in looking pretty stressed out.

'I don't even know if I'll have time to get to Asda before tea,' she says. 'I'm so behind it's not true.'

'Tough,' I say, only half listening.

'I'll die if I don't have a coffee,' Mum continues. 'How was work?'

'Good,' I say.

'You know – if you didn't mind cooking for the kids, I could pop out to Asda, then shower, and still be ready in time.'

'Yeah . . .' Something didn't add up here. As in, ready for what?

'Ready for what?'

'Oh, Jimmy! You know Steve and I are going out for

dinner – I've told you every day this week. It's Nigel's birthday. And you're babysitting.'

Everything goes into slow-motion. Nigel is Steve – my step-dad's – old schoolfriend. Yeah – I do remember Mum mentioning the fact it was his birthday. And that they were going out to celebrate. And that I said I'd babysit. Only I didn't remember that tonight was the night. A stricken look passes over my face as I *do* remember arranging to go out with Amir tonight. Hell. I don't want to cancel on him. He's my mate.

My mum reads the look on my face.

'Jimmy,' she says menacingly.

'I double-booked,' I said, looking rueful.

In an instant my mum transforms from just mum to a spitting inferno of liquid anger. It's pretty impressive.

'I just do not believe it! All week I've been on at you to remember. How often do I ask you to do something for me? Never – that's the trouble. I've spoilt you, my lad! You know, Jimmy, there *are* other people on this planet. You can't just wander aimlessly through life thinking everything will come out all right.'

Have you noticed when parents have a go at you they're never satisfied with just letting you know what you've done wrong, but they also have to assassinate your general character?

'Well, what are you going to do?'

'Mmm . . . can we pay for a babysitter and I'll go halves?'

'With what? A donation from your private income? And you think Steve and I can afford a babysitter on top of the

34

restaurant? Forget it! I'll ring Nigel and Julie and tell them we can't make it.'

That's the guilt trip. She wants me to step in and stop her sacrificing herself.

'Don't do that. I reckon Stacey is old enough to look after Kyle on her own. You're always saying she's more sensible than me anyway.' (Had to get that one in!)

'Jimmy, she's *ten*, for heaven's sake! It's against the law. Where are you going, anyway?'

'A curry with Amir, then a film.'

She's silent now and I know what she's thinking. That I ought to cancel. She reckons my life isn't as important as hers. But she won't say it. She'll beat around the bush.

'You did promise me first.'

'I forgot, OK?'

I'm a bit sharp with her but that's because I'm getting rattled now. It's not that she doesn't have a case – she does – but it's the *way* she speaks to me. She lectures me, know what I'm saying? It's like I'm still a kid and she's Mrs Know-it-all. It's the tone of her voice – long-suffering, dripping with contempt.

'Ring Amir and postpone till tomorrow,' she says now.

This annoys me even more. I am seventeen – I have a life of my own. My mum doesn't have the right to tell me what to do any more. Up till this point I was thinking about blowing out on Amir, but not now. Now there's an issue at stake here.

'I can't let a friend down.'

'Nor can we,' Mum hisses.

I realise now that both Kyle and Stacey are watching us like we're a real-life soap. Kyle's sucking his thumb and Stacey has that wide-eyed innocent look. That kills me, the way the kids are gawping at us. So I wink at them both and smile. This doesn't seem to have the right effect on my mother.

'Jimmy!' she yells like a banshee. 'You just can't take anything seriously! I can't stand the way you fool around all the bloody time – you brainless idiot! I'm going to . . . I tell you what . . . you're grounded!!'

Grounded? Yeah, right! I am seventeen! And I'm not a brainless idiot! Is that what she thinks of me? The living room, the kids are a blur and there's just me and her. I feel the weight of her hatred. I fill with rage and I don't like this feeling, don't like it at all. It scares me. I don't know what to do with the anger that swishes this way and that, boiling and bubbling. I want to hit or throw something, but I won't. I don't know how to get back to being me again. I feel my face distort and for a split second I almost think I'm going to cry. But that wouldn't look good in the movie.

'I'm going out,' I say. 'You can't stop me.'

'Wait till I tell Steve!'

'Steve won't do anything,' I remind her. 'Anyway, he's got no right to.'

'He's been as much a father to you as . . .'

My mum's voice fades away. We're both entering dangerous territory here. Two of us in a tussocky wasteland full of landmines. I only half belong to this family and she knows it. So do I. We're not supposed to mention this, ever.

Stacey cries, 'Stop it, both of you!'

We both stare at her. I'm still seething and don't trust myself to stay in control. So I push past her and leave the room. I feel in my pocket and I've got my keys, my cashcard, my phone and some loose change. I walk out the front door – slamming it loud – and think, that'll serve her right. But at the same time I feel as guilty as hell.

I stamp down to the main road where I can get a train or bus back into the city. I see and hear nothing around me as I tussle with my feelings. I'm not happy, and I hardly understand why that whole scene took place. The truth is, I'm one of those people who only knows how to feel good – I can't do any other state. Though I think my mum is unfair and I don't understand why she hates me, I don't like thinking about her having to cancel. I get an idea. I ring Lisa, a mate from college. She lives round the corner. I ask her if she'll babysit but tell her the babysitting is a present from me to my mum and I'll pay her. She's really pleased to do it as she loves kids and wants to be a nursery nurse. She's *so* pleased I wonder if she fancies me, but I decide to think about that another time. I give her Mum's number and tell her to ring her now to tell her she's coming round.

Damn. I'll have to borrow some more cash off Amir to pay her, but my wages come through on Monday so I can give him an instalment of my debt then.

I'm calming down now, getting back into my natural rhythm. A bus comes; I jump on it and make my way to the back where there's a window seat. Look, I just don't understand why my mum's got it in for me like that. OK, I admit there was a problem about the babysitting, granted, but you'd have thought we could have discussed it like two adults, rather than her going into screaming mode immediately. Either she's got a problem like PMT or something, or for some reason she's permanently pissed off with me. Like I shouldn't be there. Like she and Steve and the kids make up the perfect family and I'm surplus to requirements.

This kind of cheers me up. There's basically a movie in this struggling to get out. I'm the victim/hero, and then I have to have a series of adventures like in a road movie to prove myself. I'll run away with a sidekick – Amir? Sophie? – and travel the country in a clapped-out old car, nearly losing my life on several occasions. And meeting groups of weird people – like that bar in *Star Wars* – yeah! Meanwhile Mum and Steve are beside themselves and send out a party looking for me, and they keep missing me. Nicole Kidman could play my mum, except Mum's a bit podgier than her. Nicole could always put on a fat suit or something. I like it.

I get into town early and wander round a bit. Though it's still light the shops are shut and only the pubs and restaurants have their doors open. I love the way everything looks so solid in the dying light. I get a rush of excitement for no reason from nowhere. This is where I want to be – in the city – with night coming on. I cross the square in front of the town hall to the curry house in the basement that Amir reckons is worth checking out.

He's waiting outside; we greet each other and walk down the stairs to the huge dining area with those long refectory-style tables and loads of eager waiters ushering you in. We go to the eat-as-much-as-you-can buffet and load our plates. We both shovel food in – I realise I'm starving. The curries are good and I wipe my plate with the moon-shaped remnant of my naan bread.

We talk about what film to see. Amir's quite keen on the new Pixar movie, but I'm in the mood for something a bit more arty. There's an award-winning Italian film about these kids struggling with poverty in a village near Naples, and the price the heroine pays for selling out.

'But it'll be in subtitles, man,' Amir says, looking baffled.

I shrug. 'The lead is supposed to be quite a babe.'

'Yeah, but – not many laughs, innit.'

'That suits me,' I say and Amir picks up on my mood now. He's a decent bloke – everyone likes him at Coffee Corp. He's always looking out for ways to help people.

'You not feeling so good?' he asks me.

'My mum's giving me grief.'

'She's got it in for you?' Amir looks concerned.

'Yeah, you know what mums are like.' But as I say that I realise Amir doesn't have my problems. I've met his mum a few times when I've been round at his place. Big lady, wears a headscarf, always smiling. She's quite a bit older than my mum – Amir's the youngest of five. She mainly cooks and chats to you when you come round. She's like a real mum, solid, dependable, there for you. I concede this to Amir.

'But your mum's different. She's all right.'

Amir grins. 'Yeah – I love my mum.' He says it easily and I'm jealous of him. 'What's yours been up to, then?'

'It's just like I can't do anything right. She is seriously pissed off with me all the time.'

'Man!' Amir says, sympathetically. I drain my lager and feel like talking. My mate Amir's a good audience.

'What you've got to understand,' I tell him, 'is that I'm not really part of the family. Steve is just my step-dad – he's all right and that – leaves me alone most of the time. But the kids, Stacey and Kyle, they're just my half-sister and -brother. When my mum was a student she got pregnant with me. She was only young. It was at someone's party and she'd had too much to drink. So she had this one-night stand – the next morning this bloke had gone. She reckons he was probably a gatecrasher. When she realised she was pregnant, she decided to keep the baby – me.'

'That's some story!' Amir says, appreciatively.

'It is,' I agree.

'So you don't know your dad at all?'

'Nope. And I don't want to.' Because I feel he's not part of who I really am. He's this shadowy, unreal figure and it surprises me how little I've thought about him.

'Hey, listen, Jimmy. You need cheering up. There's a party tomorrow night. This girl I know – Natalie, man – it's her eighteenth. She's got a free house and she told me to bring who I like. You up for it?'

'I'll see how I feel,' I tell him. Of course I'm going to the party, but right now I'm into being this tragic figure. People like Amir who give you loads of sympathy make you act up like that.

We both cast our eyes back to the buffet and wonder if we

40

can get any more down us. Maybe not. Time for the movie.

After we pay I nick one of those mint imperials they have in a tray by the till, and with my mouth full, I ask Amir which of his mates are joining us.

'None of 'em, man.'

'But you said . . .'

'Yeah, but they changed their mind. They're staying at home with Mo's sister.'

'Why's that?' I ask, moving the mint from one side of my mouth to the other.

'She was upset. These blokes keep having a go at her in the street.'

'What do you mean?' We're outside now, on our way to the cinema, striding along, side by side.

'Couple of times, this car's been seen down their road, with an England flag on the front, hooting, and kerb-crawling, and shouting racist stuff.'

'Idiots.'

'Then this afternoon two of them blokes pushed past Zahira when she was coming back from work, and pulled off her headscarf.'

'That's tight! Did they hurt her, or . . . ?'

'No, but she was well upset.'

'Do I know her, this Zahira?'

'Zahira Khan. She's back from uni.'

'She used to go to my college! I wouldn't fancy mucking around with her. She had a bit of a mouth on her. Even the teachers kept away.'

'Yeah I know but she's upset now, right.'

I want to cheer him up and show him I care. 'Forget it. Ignore them and they'll go away. Or get the police on the case.'

'We have – the police say they can't do anything. These blokes aren't there long enough for them to get a car over there.'

I'm sympathetic, but a bit surprised by the whole thing. I never think of Amir as any different to me. These days, we don't care what colour people are, or what race they are. Like, in Coffee Corp, Amir's Asian and Charlene's half-Jamaican, Liz is an alien . . . I chuckle to myself. And moving on from us, there's Will Smith and Halle Berry and Spike Lee's *Do The Right Thing* – that was a cool movie. Not to mention *East Is East* and *Bend It Like Beckham*.

'Tell you what,' I say to Amir. 'You and me will stake them out. We can hide behind your garden hedge, and when the car drives past, we'll open fire, spray them with a volley of bullets. Splatter the insides of their heads all over the upholstery.'

Amir looks dubious.

'Like in *Pulp Fiction*?'

'You got it.'

I'm pleased with myself. In my head I've dealt with those racists. I've used the power of the movies to exterminate them. They're dead. Really dead. Blown into smithereens. And best of all, my mate Amir knows I'm on his side.

We get to the cinema and join the queue that snakes round and round the foyer. I inhale the mixed-up sweet and savoury aroma of popcorn and hot dogs, I see the pick 'n' mix counter with multicoloured sweets like jewels. I scan the line of posters for details of coming attractions. There's so much to look forward to. I fill with happy anticipation.

Yeah, this is the life! This is *my* life.

LIZ'S DIARY

Sunday 29th July

Third entry

Oh, my God – what have I done?

That was the thought I woke with this morning, and now I'm going to explain why I had it, and what happened. They say that confession is good for you and maybe I need to see all this in writing. Then I can decide how bad it really all is.

I went to a party last night – but no – that isn't really where it all began, although it's where it happened. It started earlier, when I got back from Coffee Corp and I saw Peter's car outside our house.

Well, she hasn't wasted any time, I thought.

I let myself in, walked down the hall to our sitting room and there he was, relaxing on our settee, a mug of coffee in his hand, and Maggie was sitting by his feet on the floor, like a big kid or something. I looked around for suitcases or bags, but there were none. I wondered what he was doing here.

They both got up and now I really looked at Peter – as if I'd never seen him before. The first thing I noticed were his hairy arms! He was wearing a short-sleeved shirt, and what a mistake! Because of those hairy arms. Like an ape. Then the next thing I remembered was that he was shorter than her. The top of his head came up to about her ears.

This kind of made me feel better. It was so obvious Maggie and him didn't fit together. A short bloke with hairy arms! He shook my hand and his was warm and almost slippery. Maggie rushed out to the kitchen to get me a drink and left us to it.

'How was work?' Peter asked.

'OK,' I said. 'I only did the afternoon as I had an early yesterday.'

'I expect you're busy, being right in the centre of the city.'

'Not especially on a Saturday.'

Those were the words we spoke, or something like them. I don't really need to recall them exactly. But really we were both thinking entirely different things. He was scanning my face, smiling shyly, glancing over to the kitchen as if Maggie was *his* mum or something, and I'm thinking, how could my mum fall in love with *you*? He wasn't bad looking – his face was OK – his eyes were kind – and he had short, curly hair, well cut. His shirt was a pale blue Ben Sherman. But there was just something very weird about him.

No – not weird – he was normal enough for a bloke. It's hard to put this into words. He looked out of place, like he shouldn't have been in our room with my mum. He was all right – friendly and that – but he didn't match Maggie. She came back into the room, carrying a glass of orange juice for me, in her beige T-shirt and black combats – and her slippers as we have a pale carpet – her pink, fluffy slippers – my mum – but there was this strange man in the front room – and she wanted him to move in with us. And share her bed.

I wanted to giggle – I wanted to giggle really badly, but I hope the grin that was plastered across my face just made me look as if I was in a good mood. I watched mum sit back on the floor and so I sat at the other end of the settee to Peter. I noticed he blushed very slightly. I just prayed Maggie wouldn't move any closer to him and touch him. But she didn't, fortunately.

'Are you going out tonight?' Maggie asked.

I said I was and explained that Amir had invited me to a party a friend of his was having – a girl called Natalie. It wasn't that far from here. I didn't explain that Sophie had called in again and that Amir had invited her too, at Jimmy's prompting.

'That's cool,' Peter said.

Cool? What a creepy word for a grown man to use! Was he trying to impress me? To show me how in touch he was with the younger generation? Maggie just smiled at him and he smiled back at her. I flinched. It was like there was an invisible dotted line connecting them, a silken thread, something private and personal. It was the way they glanced at each other. It made me feel alone.

So I got up and explained that I was hot and sweaty and needed a shower and it was nice meeting him, stuff like that. Now Maggie's eyes darted anxiously at me but I smiled blandly at her. All that smiling going on, and none of us really happy or comfortable.

I went upstairs thinking that there was nothing wrong with Peter – nothing that I could put my finger on – except he didn't fit – he didn't go with my mother. They were like two totally different things put together – a cat and a cucumber – or liver and meringue. I just couldn't imagine us all being a happy threesome.

Even though this is a diary I'm not going to go on about all my preparations for the party and how I tried on everything in my wardrobe twice and put on way too much make-up and made arrangements with my mum. That kind of stuff is boring. So I got out around nine, walked for ten minutes or so, found the house where the party was and rang the bell. I don't mind going places by myself, as long as I know someone who's there.

Luckily, when the door was opened I noticed Amir in the hall. He spotted me, explained who I was, and ushered me in, along with the bottle of red wine Maggie said I could take with me. Amir guided me to the kitchen where the booze was and quickly I filled a plastic cup full of something and took a big slug. I didn't fancy seeing everything in the cold light of sobriety.

That's why – now – I can only remember bits of things. Like, for example, Sophie arriving, spotting me, giving a silly little hand wave and jumping up and down. Soon she'd steered the conversation where she wanted it to go.

'They're so *nice*! You're so lucky to work with them!' Sophie exclaimed, shooting a glance at Amir and Jimmy. 'And I spoke to Bob, your manager, and he said there's a really good chance I could join you. It would be so much fun, us working together!' I noticed her perfume was clinging to me, to my clothes. It was a quality scent, but it didn't suit me.

'I like your belt,' Sophie told me, casting her eyes down to the leather belt I'd selected, with its oversized buckle. 'Where did you get it?'

I mentioned the second-hand shop me and Maggie check out sometimes.

'That is so clever of you, knowing where to look! I just end up having to buy designer gear and paying way too much. But anyway, tell me about Amir and Jimmy – all the goss!'

I smiled at her. 'There is none.'

'Oh, come on! Like, are they both single?'

'To the best of my knowledge.'

With that information, she pushed her way over to them. I think I started dancing then with some people I knew. But soon enough Sophie was back by my side, her eyes aglow.

'He is so cute!' she informed me.

'Who is?'

'Jimmy. And he really likes you!'

'Me?' I said. My stomach gave a lurch. I hadn't expected that. The party suddenly went out of focus. I listened to Sophie intently.

'Yeah. I mean, he says you're a really good mate, a good laugh. Oh, he doesn't fancy you or anything – you're not his type – but he likes working with you.'

'Oh, right,' I said, flustered. And feeling slightly sick. Sophie vanished again.

So there we are. He didn't fancy me. Lesson learned. And worse still was the fact he told Sophie that. At the time I tried not to let it upset me, though. I just had another drink. I told myself nothing had changed – I'd never imagined he fancied me. And I wasn't even supposed to fancy him. I really had to get the whole thing with Jimmy out of my system, once and for all. It would serve me right and do me good if he got it together with Sophie.

The next thing I remember is dancing like crazy with a group of girls to some heavy metal. I was going mental, absolutely wild. Then, when I went upstairs to the bathroom, the stairs were loaded with snogging couples. I came down and decided I didn't want to dance any more so I went out into the garden.

It was only slightly cooler out there. Natalie had a huge garden, and it ended in some shrubs and bushes in the distance. The day had faded so everything looked blurred and grey. But golden light spilled out from the house and made the three blokes who stood on the decking with bottles of lager look like a reasonable proposition. I went over and introduced myself.

'I'm Liz,' I said. 'I don't know you.'

They said who they were but I couldn't hear much of what they were telling me. The music thumped out bass, people's voices rose and fell, and I had to brush my face repeatedly to get rid of the tiny insects that had landed on my cheek. They were in my hair too. I thought, I'm not really having a good time, and I wondered about cutting my losses and going home – then I remembered – Maggie might be at home –

with Peter – so I asked one of the blokes to get me another drink from the kitchen.

When he returned with a large glass of wine in a plastic cup the other two guys made their excuses and went. Which left two of us. I could see the way things were going and found I didn't mind. When I drink, it's as if all the locked doors in my head that stop me doing stuff just fly open, and I get reckless. I gave this bloke the once-over.

He wore a grey T-shirt which hung loose over some low-slung jeans – you could see his paunch pressing against the T. His hair was short and cut respectably close to his ears – I guessed he probably worked in an office – he seemed a bit older than me. Altogether, he wasn't bad looking. I mean, I wanted him not to be bad looking. The booze and my desire to have someone – anyone – was distorting my vision. When he turned out to be Natalie's older brother I was pleased. He was both safe and dangerous, if you know what I mean.

I could tell he was up for it, and we joked and flirted and I got that rush of adrenaline you do when you know something is going to happen. All the voices in my head were shouting, why not? Go for it! So I moved nearer to him, flashed my eyes at him, the usual routine. And he said all the right things, like how gorgeous I was and how he couldn't help himself but he was going to have to kiss me. And I was glad he did because I think if he hadn't put his arms round me then, I might have fallen over.

I'd pulled. That was all right, then. And to make it better still, Jimmy came out at that moment and clocked me with this guy. Which will show him that *some* guys fancy me! After a while my bloke took me by the hand and we walked through the garden. It got darker as we left the house behind. Just before the shrubbery was a small garden shed and he led me behind that. I was happy then. To be honest, I wanted someone to hug and kiss me a bit. I needed to feel the pressure of somebody's desire – the warmth and hardness of someone else, the darkness, the forgetting.

So he pushed me up against the back of the garden shed where we were out of anyone's view. We snogged for a while and then, predictably, his hands started exploring. When it got too much I started removing them. But this bloke wasn't easily deterred. He just kept putting them back again, and his big, slobbery lips were all over me. Finally he took my hand, and tried to force it down his jeans. Enough was enough. I broke away.

'Watch it,' I said.

He wasn't going to give up.

'You know you want it, baby,' he muttered, his voice slurred. He unbuttoned his jeans and then lunged at me.

I started pummelling him with my closed fists. I was angry – but even more, I was scared. He got hold of both my fists in his large paws and laughed.

'You want it rough?' he asked.

I could not believe it! Was this guy from the Stone Age or something? I could hardly credit this happening. I recalled Maggie telling me that if ever I was in trouble then a knee in the groin would do the trick. So with all the force I could muster, I lifted my knee and it connected hard and fast with that soft, squashy area I was aiming for. Success. He loosened his grip on me and bellowed with pain.

I was so angry – I don't even understand why now. I know I should have just left him then, but I didn't.

'Blokes like you make me sick!' I shouted at him. 'Just going in and taking what you want. You're so bloody irresponsible. You dickhead – you wanker – you . . .' I ran out of words and even though he was doubled over I kicked him on his shins. Again and again and again. He actually shouted for help then. A grown man shouting for help – can you believe it? I wanted to get hold of him and shake some sense into him, but I knew that would be madness. And anyway, I heard footsteps then, and someone shouting, what the heck's going on? And it was Jimmy.

'Get that woman off me!' the bloke on the ground shouted.

'Liz?' Jimmy questioned.

'You asshole,' I said as my parting shot. 'And you too,' I told Jimmy. 'You're an asshole. And so is everyone on this planet.' And I stumbled up the garden, into the house, through, and out of it, into the street and, in defiance of the rules about personal safety, walked home alone.

And here's a strange thing. On my way back, I could have sworn I spotted that man who was in Coffee Corp the other day, eyeing Jimmy. He was standing under a street light at the end of the road. But I was in such a state I guess I was hallucinating or something.

So that's how bad it was. I went to a party and got involved in a fight, beating up the hostess's brother, a guy twice my size. Half of me feels thoroughly ashamed, but the other half thinks, why not? He deserved it. And at the time, it felt good.

The worst thing, though, is going to be facing Jimmy and Amir tomorrow morning at Coffee Corp. I can just imagine the teasing. But the good thing is, I think I've finally burnt out the last traces of my feelings for Jimmy. As if he could fancy me now. He's more likely to duck when he sees me coming. Liz Burns, heavyweight champion of the world.

JIMMY

It's half eleven Monday morning and I'm totally spaced out. I've had too little sleep. These early shifts are killing me. Already this morning I've knocked over a jug of milk and tripped on the rubber mat by the bar. I'm standing at the bar now. I'm watching the two lines of espresso fill up the twin shot glasses, dancing like mice tails. Each trickles to its conclusion and the shot glasses stand there like two mini pints of beer just pulled. I watch the creamy head form on the top and the way the body darkens and the coffee settles.

'Jimmy?' Charlene's voice. Bob's at head office so she's running the joint this morning. 'You're half asleep. Take your break now.'

So I finish off the lattes, pouring in the milk, holding back the foam with the tongue-like metal spoon, and go and sit back of house for a while.

In my mind I'm replaying the movie I watched last night – one of those sword-fighting Chinese epic yarns with beautiful females with icy stares flying through the air and slashing at you. Kind of sexy. Sexy makes me think of Sophie and I'd text her again except my fingers are too tired to hit the right keys. That babe fancies me. I'm in there. We've been texting on and off since the party and I'm taking her to the movies in a few days. She is definitely the best thing right now. Then I think about slow-motion and the way all the fight scenes were slowed r – i – g – h – t down. Why does slo-mo give the impression of speed? That's a puzzle.

The door of the back room opens and in comes Liz. I brighten immediately. This is what I've been looking forward to all morning. I could just imagine Liz in a martial arts movie – she'd slaughter everyone in sight. She's changing into her work shoes which she's taking out of the locker.

'Hi, Rambo,' I greet her.

'Piss off,' she says.

'Can I be your manager? I can set up a bout with—'

'He had it coming, OK?'

'Maybe, but we had to take the bloke to casualty. Mild concussion.'

I love the way Liz looks appalled. I push it a bit further.

'And stitches in his shins.'

'Stitches!'

'Twenty stitches, a ruptured spleen, two broken ribs and they say he'll never be able to father children.'

'You bastard! And I believed you.'

I cower as if I'm terrified of her. She's spitting fire. This is fun. I'm still thinking of the martial arts babe but seeing Liz's face.

My phone vibrates and I check it. 'Sophie,' I tell Liz. She shoots me another glance so evil I'm scared I might have really upset her. So I try to change tack and get matey.

'We're going out next week. She's cool.'

'How nice,' Liz says, ties on her apron, and goes out front, which is where I should be now. I thought she'd be pleased I was dating her mate. I remembered telling Sophie how much I liked Liz – said she was wicked to work with, which is true. It kills me, the way she takes everything so seriously. Just the opposite of me.

I go out and get ready for the lunchtime rush. Charlene puts me on the till while Liz is at the bar. It's just one customer after another – I'm pressing in lattes, happy frappés, cappuccinos, till my fingers are sore. Then I'm at the panini grill toasting a ham and cheese panini – slam the lid shut, watch the red digits count down. I'm deafened by Charlene grinding coffee next to me – as bad as Mum vacuuming the living room. A picture comes into my head of my mum and the way she's not properly talking to me still. But that's better than the constant sniping I usually get from her. It's unbearably hot in here – the panini grill pumps out the heat. *Beep*, *beep*. Sandwich ready – flattened into submission, melted cheese licking from its middle, dripping onto the grill. I lift each half with the scraper and slide it on a plate. And a chocolate muffin from the ambient display counter. Bob's back, his apron's on, and he joins me at the till.

And then it's two, the end of my shift. In a few moments I'm out of Coffee Corp and thinking I'll go to the bank and check if my wages have come through. So I'm walking along the busy street, cut through an alley to Exchange Square where the hole in the wall is. There's a queue. I join it. And I'm about to go back to the movie in my head, the scene on the sand dunes, when . . .

Someone taps me on the shoulder.

I turn and the bloke behind me says, 'Hello.'

Like a camera my eyes snap his face, and my brain registers it as known, familiar. I frown as I try to place him. It's the guy who came in on Friday, the one who kept staring at me. I'm immediately on my guard.

'Yeah?'

'It's Jimmy, isn't it?'

I admit it is, and I'm glad Exchange Square is full of people, otherwise I might not have disclosed my identity. Our voices are low and the other people in the queue aren't paying any attention. The bloke asks if he can have a word with me and almost against my will I find myself moving out of the line, and position myself close to the wall of the bank, and he faces me.

'Jimmy,' he says, his voice a little unsteady. 'I'm your father.'

I don't take this in. Steve is my dad. Well, no, in actual fact he isn't but ... This doesn't make sense and the only thought in my mind is to get more information. What is this bloke on about? I ask him what he means.

'I'm your dad,' he repeats, his lips forming a shy smile. 'Mike Sanderson.'

I've never heard that name before in my life. But then, why would I? My mum's told me the story of how she met my biological father – how she had too much to drink and that – but she never mentioned his name. Now I come to think of it, she even said she didn't remember his name.

'You're having me on,' I say to this bloke, Mike. Now I'm thinking this is a wind-up – Liz's revenge for what I did to her earlier – and I don't want to seem an idiot. She's probably waiting round the corner.

'You've had your fun,' I say. 'Now push off.'

'Jimmy,' he pleads. 'I just want to talk to you for a few minutes.'

In the distance a street musician starts up on the sax. It forms a wistful soundtrack. I should have walked away quickly but I didn't.

'I can see this might have come as a shock to you,' this Mike says. 'I couldn't think of any other way of introducing myself. Do you want to sit down?'

He indicates a bench under a tree which is empty. I decline the offer.

'How much has Carol told you?' Mike persists.

Hearing him speak my mum's name gave me a shock. It proved a connection between them.

'Enough,' I say.

'She still uses her maiden name,' he comments. 'That was how I traced her. So she's single?'

She's not – she's married to Steve. But my mum kept her maiden name – Keane – as she was using it for her beautician business. I decide this bloke needed to know she was with someone, in case he's planning anything tricky.

'She's married,' I tell him.

He nods slowly. I half think I'll wake up in a moment and find out I'm dreaming all of this. None of it is making any real sense. This man, Mike – he's dressed very tidily, his shirt is crisp and looks new. He's wearing a dark blue silk tie. His hair's greying and cut close to his ears. He seems respectable. He looks as if he wants to carry on talking, carry on telling me things.

'I hope she's been fair in what she's said to you. The most important thing is that you know I never left you. That was not my choice. I would have taken you with me, but she took you before I could stop her. There just turned out to be . . . a high degree of incompatibility. That was all.'

What the hell is he talking about?

'I don't get you,' I snarl at him.

Once again he beckons to the empty bench. This time I follow him over there as I find my legs are weak. This bloke – Mike – gives me the willies but my curiosity is stronger than my fear. I have to hear what he's going to say. He's probably a complete loony, but I'll have fun telling Liz and Amir and everyone. It's freaky – and just a bit cool – to have your own stalker. Here I am joking about it, because I don't know how else to react.

He hitches his trousers as he sits, and straightens them. I sit far away from him.

'How much do you know, Jimmy?'

I debate with myself whether to tell him, but in the end I do. Because there wasn't that much to say. I explain about Mum getting drunk and that she couldn't trace my dad. Mike goes very still. There's a pause, followed by a silence.

'That's not true,' he says.

'It's what she told me.'

He looks at me with a fierce intensity that makes me shudder. You know that expression 'his eyes blazed'? Well, his are black and blazing.

'No. That's not what happened. I met your mother when she was nineteen. It was love at first sight. We were at a club and it was getting late. I was on my way out when I saw her. I knew there and then we were meant for each other. It wasn't a romantic feeling – more a sense of inevitability. She knew it too. We got engaged after a month. Her parents were wary but they couldn't object. I had a steady job – I could afford the rent on our own place.' He stops and scans my face to see how I'm taking all this. I'm fine. It's like he's talking about complete strangers. I could be watching a film. I *am* watching a film – a film within a film. I'm the audience and he's the action. The inside of my head is the screen. I listen – and watch the images unfold – as he talks.

He tells me how they married after just four months. So I see them standing together in the registry office, a lady registrar in front of them conducting the ceremony, light pouring in through the window. He says they didn't have a honeymoon – they didn't need one as they were so much in love. Now there's him and my mum, stopping on the pavement, newly married, turning to gaze lovingly at each other, embracing. My mum, not much older than me.

Time passes. They've been married for a few months. I see them in a cramped flat in a box-like kitchen with cracked linoleum on the floor. He's telling me they stopped getting on so well. They're arguing most of the time. She's saying she needs to get out more, that she's tired of being trapped in the flat with him. He's saying she's wrong, that he should be all she ever needed. 'Maybe I love you too much,' he's saying to her. 'More than you love me.'

In the next scene she's lit up with happiness again. She gets up, turns off the telly in the flat, in a room with flowery wallpaper, and perches on the side of the armchair he's sitting in. She puts a hand on his arm. She tells him that she's pregnant. With me. He says she was sick quite badly. I see her bent over the sink in the bathroom. He's outside the bathroom door, looking pained and concerned. Split-screen effect here.

He tells me when I was born it was the best day of his life. He's standing by my mum who's in bed, in hospital, and he's cradling me in his arms, gazing at me tenderly. She's looking on with pride. Or is she holding me? Is he looking at us? Whatever. We're a family. Total, complete, self-contained. The nurse who's coming in with a tray of food hesitates in the door, unwilling to disturb the composition. Me, my mum and my dad. Like Jesus, Mary and Joseph. No – that's all wrong – I try Travolta, Kirstie Alley and the kid from *Look Who's Talking*. The baby is voiced by Bruce Willis. That's me.

I bring my attention back. Mike says the arguments started again. She's depressed because I'm screaming all the time. He's telling her to get herself together. One night his dinner's not ready. He asks her what she's been doing all day. She tries talking to him nicely but he gives her the silent treatment. I'm screaming for attention because I need changing, because my needs are ignored.

Then he delivers the climax – the key scene – the one it's all been leading up to. The day he gets back from work and she's gone – gone without even telling him. He's distraught,

61

shouting her name in a frenzy. Carol! CAROL!! How could you do this to me? You never even gave me a chance to explain, a chance to change my ways. He cries molten tears of agony and self-reproach.

Time passes. He fights back. He tells me he joins the army. Yeah – one morning, on an impulse, as the wind whips up the rubbish on the pavement, he heads into an army recruitment office and stands to attention at the desk. He wants to forget. It's like joining the foreign legion, it's like *Lawrence of Arabia*. Or maybe *Platoon* . . . or *Black Hawk Down*. Then he's accepted, he trains, he learns how to use a bayonet – I see him running at a dummy hanging from a bar – he's on a shooting range, then scrambling up some rigging on an assault course . . .

He tells me he's been abroad until recently – that's why he's not been in contact up till now. After he left the army, he settled in Cyprus. I see him at the outside table of a taverna, drinking with other ex-soldiers. His skin's deeply tanned – he's wearing a khaki short-sleeved shirt. He says he ran his own taxi business, but it wasn't challenging enough. There are a couple of his cars parked on the road – yellow sedans, saying 'Mike's Taxi Service' in black lettering.

He explains how he came back here, and joined a military security operation. He was sent to Iraq as he had no dependents – and the money was good, very good. I see newsreels in my head now, bomb-scarred streets, dust, then more dust, burning heat, sullen, embittered Iraqis. He says that out there he made some excellent friends – the best he'd ever had. I hear him telling me how the fact men are under constant pressure

62

means they form relationships quickly. He tells me about Colin. Colin is younger than me, just out of the army.

He lets me know how he took him under his wing, got him out of a number of scrapes. I see this Colin foolishly taunting some Iraqis, insulting their religion – or have I got mixed up with those newspaper pictures of British soldiers abusing prisoners? Weren't they all made up anyway? I tune into Mike's story again.

He describes how one day – a Tuesday morning – they were guarding an oil installation. I watch him in uniform, in front of a complicated series of metallic tanks and sealed-off enclosures. It's hot, white-hot. You can see nothing clearly because of the glare and the dust. He says the woman who came up to them was a beggar, her hand was outstretched. They'd recognised her because she'd been hanging around for days. Filthy woman – foul and stinking, he says. He shooed her away. That's when she thrust her hand in her skirts and pulled out the bomb. She threw it directly at Colin. The explosion deafens and the screen judders. He says he never realised before how quickly you can be a human being one moment, and then be nothing, just a mess on the ground.

A mess on the ground. Spilled guts, a pool of black blood. Even my mind shies away from that. So I listen to his voice again, real time.

He explains how it affected him very badly, as Colin had been like a son to him. Why do I feel a sudden spurt of jealousy? But now he tells me how much he'd thought of me and that he bitterly regretted the years he'd missed. He came back here to find me, to have a son again. His real son. He'd traced my mum on the Internet – she'd signed up to a website for old pupils from her school. She'd said she was living in this city. He came here and went to the local library and there was an advertisement for her business, with our address. He found me and followed me. Because he knows just a little about surveillance. His voice trails away.

The final credits roll. I don't know what I think. It's a rubbish movie. Doesn't make sense. I don't believe any of it.

Now I look in Mike's face. There are the scars I remember seeing – feathery indentations on his forehead and on one cheek. From the bomb that killed his friend? I see my eyes in his eyes, my chin in his chin. I'm icy cold although the day is hot. A small part of me is resisting all of this and saying that this Mike is a nutter. The rest of me knows he's telling the truth, *a* truth. But why hadn't Mum told me any of this? That was what didn't add up.

'This is a lot for you to take in,' Mike says, gently.

I'm as still as a statue. A girl arrives and stands by the bench. Mike shifts up so there's room for her. I back away as he nears me.

'I understand if you need time.' Mike speaks softly. I see the way his chest rises and falls. 'Let me give you my card. It's got my mobile number, and my address. I'm renting a flat in the city centre. Park Point. Do you know it? When you feel ready, contact me. I'll be waiting. I don't want to put any pressure on you. Speak to your mother first – she'll confirm what I've told you. And if there's anything – anything – I can do for you – you just have to say. You're my son, my flesh and blood.'

That sax again, mournful, insistent. The aroma of the girl's chicken salsa sandwich. I feel ill. Mike gets up then and puts out his hand. I shake it. His grip is firm but somehow respectful of me – I don't know. I don't know anything any more. I watch him walk away through the crowd in the direction of Park Point. I know where he means. It's an exclusive development of apartments and duplexes, in the redeveloped area down near the canal.

I don't know what to do now because nothing seems real any more, nothing at all.

LIZ'S DIARY

Monday 30th July

Fourth entry

I still haven't said anything to Maggie about Peter.

This morning, I'd decided I needed some help. Maybe if I spoke to someone, they'd advise me. Someone a little older than me. Someone like Charlene. So when it had quietened down at Coffee Corp and Charlene and I stopped for a moment or two, I bit my lip, took a deep breath and prepared myself. I was washing my hands at the sink. Charlene asked me how my weekend had been. That was my cue.

'Guess what,' I said, quite casual, testing the words, seeing what they sounded like. 'My mum asked me if her boyfriend could move in with us.' I dried my hands carefully.

'Wicked!' Charlene said. 'She's been divorced for ages, hasn't she?'

I agreed. Charlene grinned at me. 'Good for her. What's he like? Have you met him?'

I felt myself withdraw and shrivel. 'He's OK. A journalist at the *Courier*.' I tried to think of an objection to him so Charlene would end up on my side. 'I think he's a bit younger than her.'

'A toy boy! Better still. You go, girl! What can I get you? Liz – two cappuccinos and an iced tea.'

Just for a second I wanted to cry, but the feeling passed. I knew I shouldn't be angry with Charlene – she couldn't help missing the point. I wanted her to see it from my point of view, and she didn't. Instead she made me question how fair I was being to Maggie. Was I putting my own interests first? Was I being selfish? Probably – but also inside me there's a tight knot of fear and resentment. I feel like I'm being pushed aside in some way, and the people who are pushing me are too much in love to see it. Whatever.

We got busy – three strawberry happy frappés one after the other – the frappé maker banging and crushing the ice as if it was a bag of nails in there – and the noise stopped me thinking, until it was time for a break. Bob was back by then, so it was OK for me to go out for a bit. I thought I'd walk around and get my head together. It sucks, feeling bad when the weather's good. The sunshine made even the buildings look happy, office workers stood around in short-sleeve shirts smoking, girls were dressed in bright colours, but I felt as if I was carrying my personal cloud around with me, grey, oppressive and suffocating. That self-pitying mood was choking me like a vice. I mooched into Exchange Square and passed the guy on the sax. He was good. I added to the coins in his hat. As I moved away I looked over to the tree in the centre, and saw Jimmy alone on the bench underneath it.

I was glad to see him. He hadn't given me a hard time about the fight, and his wind-up was quite funny, in a way. Perversely I felt more angry with Charlene just now. Then I remembered that I'd meant to speak to Jimmy about the fact I'd seen that bloke hanging round outside Natalie's party. I approached him.

'I thought you'd be on your way home by now,' I started.

'Yeah,' he replied. His voice was flat, he didn't look me in the eyes. Something was wrong with him. My own bad mood vanished in an instant, changing into concern.

'What's up, Jimmy?'

He didn't respond. I wasn't sure what to do. So I sat by him and said nothing for a while. Then I explained about the bloke I'd seen.

'I'm sure it was him. Hanging around outside in the street. Creepy, isn't it?'

'Just lay off,' he said to me. 'Drop it, OK?'

I was shocked. His voice was rough and aggressive. Jimmy had never, ever spoken to me – or to anyone – like that before. I backed away.

'Sorry,' I said.

'Me too. Look, I don't feel too good. Something's come up.'

'Can I help?'

'No – it's nothing. It's probably all a load of lies. There are some pretty strange people around. I'll be OK. I just need a good night's sleep.'

'You're babbling,' I told him.

'Yeah. Ignore me. See you later.' And he got up and walked away.

I couldn't make head nor tail of his behaviour. Was it something I'd done? Or maybe Sophie was giving him a hard time. I was floundering, and I knew it. When I went back to Coffee Corp, I asked Charlene if she knew what was up, but she said he was fine, just a bit knackered. So maybe that was it. I picked up the blue plastic tray to go and collect the empties from out front.

I got home about eight thirty and it was my turn to be knackered. I joined Maggie on the sofa where she was watching a cop drama on the box. I tried to talk about my day but I could tell she wasn't listening. Her eyes were fixed on the TV screen. Great.

'I'm hungry,' I said.

'I left you some pasta. You can warm it up in the microwave.'

It flashed into my mind that some people come home from work and their dinner is waiting for them, or their mum will hurry into the kitchen herself and warm up the pasta. So I sighed and rolled my eyes, not bothering whether she saw me or not. I didn't get up off the sofa. After a few moments, when the action on telly subsided, she said, 'Go on, then. You said you were hungry.'

'Not for pasta.'

'There's not much else in the house.'

'Whatever,' I said.

Looking back now, I can see I was trying to rile her. But I was in a bad mood and she's my mum and if you can't be in a bad mood with your own mum then who can you be in a bad mood with?

'Do you want me to heat up the pasta?' she asked.

'No, I can do it,' I replied. But I didn't do it.

Then a police car's siren blotted out our words and both of us were drawn to the screen and watched the ending of the episode. I grabbed one of the cushions and hugged it to my stomach. I didn't want pasta. I fancied chips, something comforting.

The end credits started rolling and Maggie turned to me.

'There was a fight in the office today. One of my clients. The receptionist was new and she was terrified. She ran out and back to the agency that sent her.'

'Oh,' I said.

'Liz? Are you OK?'

'Yeah – pre-menstrual,' I ad-libbed quickly.

'I had a crap day at work today,' Maggie said.

'So did I,' I countered. We seemed to be arguing and I was glad. Also, at the same time, I hated it. Does this make sense? Probably not.

'What happened to you?' Maggie asked.

'Just hassle,' I muttered.

I could feel myself getting churned up inside. I just wanted Maggie to give me a big hug and ruffle my hair like she used to. But she didn't. Instead I could feel the irritation sparking from her.

'Is there something wrong, Liz?'

I didn't like the way this situation was developing. We seemed to be on different sides of a chasm. So I decided to back off.

'It's just that I really don't fancy pasta – can we go out and get some chips, maybe? Or go to the supermarket for some ice-cream?'

I glanced at Maggie. There was a furtive look about her. She ran her fingers through her hair.

'Tell you what – we'll have a takeaway tomorrow – or even go to the cinema as well. It's just that Peter's coming round later for a bit, after his class.'

'Fine,' I said, with all the sarcasm I could muster.

'Liz,' Maggie said pleadingly. 'Don't make this awkward. For my sake.'

For her sake. That's what it's all about, isn't it? Her. What about me? Where do I fit into this? Something molten in my chest expanded and heaved. I wanted to rush out of the room, or scream, or throw something, but I knew that would put me in the wrong. I wanted to hurt her, but I didn't want to hurt her.

So I just said, 'I don't feel well,' and left the room. And that was true. I didn't feel well, not at all well.

So I came up here. And my appetite's gone. And just ten minutes or so ago I heard the doorbell chime and the sound of a visitor. It was Peter. The conversation was muted. Were they talking about me? I found some gum in my pocket and I'm just having to make do with that.

Maggie always tells people that she's never understood why people complain about teenagers. She says I never went through any awkward stage. But right now, I feel like the stroppy kid I never was. I want to hurt her. Because I don't know how to explain that it's one thing her going out with Peter, but another bringing him here and breaking up our home. Why couldn't she have waited till next year?

But I know the answer – it's because of his job. So it's up

to me to make the sacrifices, and I wish I was able to go down and tell them I'm happy with him moving in, but I can't do it. I just can't.

I'm dabbing at the tear stains on this page with a tissue but you can still see where the paper is dimpled and wrinkled with the moisture. I hate myself for getting in this state.

I wish there was another person I could turn to – someone I could talk all this through with. If I had a boyfriend – I'm trying not to think of Jimmy – maybe I wouldn't feel so alone. But it's no use thinking like that. I've got to learn to rely on myself more.

That's my resolution.

JIMMY

It needs clever editing, this film of my life, so you can see how I feel right now. Take a few quick-fire shots of me going about my everyday business – grinding coffee beans at work, inhaling the dusky brown aroma, texting my mates, brushing my teeth, even taking Sophie to the movies, edging forward in the endless queue leading to the ticket booths, and the automated voice going, *position number five, please* – just to establish my life was rolling on as usual, but then – then – the meaningful shots. The one where I pause and a dark, haunted look inhabits my face. Or one where I pull Mike's – my dad's? – card out of my pocket and look at it, wondering, trying to decide what to do. Or watching my mother bending over Kyle to help him with his handwriting and thinking, why hasn't she told me the truth? A look of distrust, puzzlement on his – my – features.

I'm editing like this all the time. It gives me space and time. It helps me come to terms with it. Either a loony has chosen me to infect with his weird fantasies about wanting a son – but then, how did he know so much about my mum? Why go to all that trouble to find me? Or my mother's lied to me. Neither is good.

I haven't told anyone any of this. Because they would

think I'm mad. Or they would tell me to speak to my mum, and I'm not ready, not yet. I just want to see what happens next. I want to be in the audience and not in the centre of the action. I want to see if Mike will carry on stalking me – because if he does, he's a nutter and I should go straight to the police. But if he doesn't, if he's happy to wait for me to contact him, then that kind of proves he's telling the truth, doesn't it? I'm testing him. So far, he's left me alone.

I keep replaying what he told me and I know it as well as if I had the DVD. A film with his voice-over – his early marriage to my mum, his time in the army and what happened to him in Iraq. That's the X-rated bit. To see your best mate blown up. I rewind again to the scene in Exchange Square and reshoot it deep focus, with the crowds and the queue and the sax player. Then I zoom in and close up on me and him. Everything else fades away.

'Jimmy? Isn't it past the end of your shift?'

'What?'

Bob's voice breaks into my thoughts.

'No home to go to?' he jokes.

I grin at him, and go back of house, glad to get out of the suffocating heat behind the bar. Thank goodness the air con is working. I take off my apron, check my watch and see it's two in the afternoon. In a few moments I'm out on the street, looking about me to see if Mike turns up again. I see only a bunch of strangers. It's stifling out here. The kind of heat that makes it hard to breathe, that forms beads of sweat on your forehead. Everyone looks tense, expectant. It's building up for a storm.

On the train back home I'm more and more certain I have the pitch for a movie here. Bloke turns up and reveals to his son that he's his true father and sparks off an identity crisis. Maybe I should save up for a ticket to LA, barge into some studio and sell my idea. It would solve all my financial worries in one stroke. And I do have financial worries. The date with Sophie set me back a bit, but it was worth it. She's probably the best-looking girl I've ever been out with. She tosses her hair like Jennifer Aniston. We didn't say much, but I can tell she seems pretty keen on me. I think. I text her now, which cheers me up, trying to arrange to meet up with her again. I look out of the window and see the sky's changed colour. It has a yellowy tinge – like in *South Pacific* when they experiment with Technicolor and turn the sky yellow ochre in the romantic bits. Every window on the train is open but the air that's blown in is stale and hot. *Dog Day Afternoon. Towering Inferno.* I try thinking of *The Day After Tomorrow* to cool me down. New York ice-bound. Mmm.

My stop. I walk slowly in the stifling heat and see the light's gone out of the sky. I try to quicken my pace so I can make it home before the rain starts. It's still dry when I reach home and unlock the front door. I can hear the sky holding its breath, waiting to scream its storm.

The house isn't empty, like I thought it would be. Mum's in the sitting room on the settee, reading a magazine.

'Oh, hi, Jimmy,' she says. 'My two thirty cancelled on me. I'm having a breather. The kids are round at Sarah's. Has it started raining yet?'

'Not yet.' I say.

And it strikes me this is a good time. The kids are at school. Steve's at work. I like the feel of the impending storm. Shall I tell her about Mike now? I feel my throat tighten and my pulse quicken. Maybe I'll just go and shower first. I stand hesitantly in the doorway.

'Come in if you're coming in, and go out if you're going out,' Mum says.

I think, that's a clumsy sentence and in the movie I'd have to change it – she'd say something like, 'Jimmy, what is it? I can sense that something's wrong between us.' I'd deny it but give away by my body language that something most definitely is wrong. Instead I carry on standing there.

'If you've got nothing to do, you can get me a Diet Coke from the fridge. And put some ice in it. Oh, and you can refill the ice tray if you use the last cubes.'

She's so unconcerned. It makes me angry, that she doesn't know about what I'm going through. I want to begin, but I find I don't know how.

'Jimmy, move, why don't you?'

I don't move. I realise that's actually the best way to begin – to alert her to the fact that things aren't normal, and will never be normal again. I'm sort of standing there with an imaginary axe in my hand, holding it above her head. I try to script my lines, but only come out with:

'Can we talk about something?'

Damn. I should have said, 'I met someone the other day. Someone from your past. And from my past as well.' Only I don't. I begin with those pathetic words, *can we talk about something?* I prefer the film version. I'm not that fond of real

76

life. It's almost as dark as night out there, but it's only mid-afternoon.

'Talk about what?' she says, putting down her magazine. She's been reading an article about suntan lotions.

One final pause – because I know what's going to happen. I'm going to tell her my story about Mike and she's going to laugh loud and long and tell me he was barking mad. That he'd told me a pack of lies. That I'd been working myself up about nothing. I'd been a fool. I needed to get a grip on real life. My fantasy – my film – would be over. A pity, really. So when I start, my voice sounds tinny and small.

'The other day this bloke came into Coffee Corp.' She's smiling at me, unconcerned. 'His name was Mike. He said he was my dad.'

I know there and then. It's the way her colour comes and goes. A look of horror crosses her face but it lasts less than a second. I see her features set into a mask and I think there's a crash of thunder outside but I might be imagining it. Both of us are scared – I don't know who's more scared. I put my hand on the doorframe for support. I carry on.

'He said he's been following me. He told me you got married to him but then you walked out on him. But I thought you didn't really know my real dad. I'm confused.'

I understand that stuff about slow-motion now. We're in slow-motion but a lot is happening. A whole chunk of what I know about myself is turning out not to be true. Mum's the person I trust most, but I feel that changing. Her voice is low as she tells me to sit down by her. I don't want to. I prefer being here, at a distance, and above her. There really is thunder and lightning now. The room is lit up for a broken instant, then is dull again.

'OK,' Mum says. 'If I didn't tell you this before, it was because I was certain it was for your own good.'

I feel sick.

'Mike was my mistake and I didn't want him to be your mistake as well. I married him when I was too young – I was convinced I was in love. I wouldn't listen to my parents. But he turned out to be . . . not good, Jimmy. I don't know how much to tell you!' She looks up at me appealingly, for guidance.

'Everything,' I say.

'There's not much more. He was . . . hard to live with. There were things about him. I don't want to . . .'

I feel like a bully. It's obvious Mum doesn't want to tell me any more. But I have a right to know. This is my life we're talking about here.

'What things?' I hear my voice rising hysterically.

'He was cruel to me. I don't want to say any more.'

'What things?'

'No, Jimmy. It's not for you to know. It's all over. Where is Mike? Here? Are you going to see him again?'

'He's living in the city.'

'Will you see him?'

'I might.'

'Oh, God!' my mum wailed. Now the rain came pelting down, crashing against the window, pouring in torrents down the glass.

I really am confused. Part of me wants to go and hug

Mum as she's in such a state. I actually want to comfort her. But she's lied to me, and I don't understand why. Also I want to know everything about Mike, I want to hear about him from her lips, but at the same time, I don't. I don't want her barging in and spoiling it. So I don't press her for more information. I just say:

'You lied to me.'

'For your sake.'

'You stopped me knowing him!' It's a kind of a relief, blaming it all on her.

'He went away.' Her eyes dart to the clock. 'I need to pick the kids up.' Then, 'Jimmy, I'm sorry. We'll talk about it later, if you like.'

'Whatever.'

I walk into the kitchen, unlock the back door, and go and stand in the garden, letting the lukewarm rain cascade over me. I'm getting soaked. My T-shirt is clinging to me. My hair is plastered to my face. I can't see out of my eyes. So I don't know whether I'm crying or not. I'm not who I think I am. I have a real dad. My mum lied to me all my life.

When you think about it, it's pretty cool. I mean, it doesn't happen to many people. I wonder what my mates will say when I tell them. I rub the rain from my eyes. And think I don't really need a shower now. I wonder how Sophie will react. To be honest, I got the impression on our date that she was only mildly interested in me. When I tell her all this, she'll be seriously amazed.

Oh no. My dad's card. It's in my pocket and my jeans are soaked. I run back inside and shove my fingers in my jeans pocket. I extract the card. The digits of his numbers are just about legible. I get out my phone and copy them both in. I'm shivering now. Then I compose a short text: *Can we meet up again? Jimmy.* In a sweet burst of adrenaline, I press 'send'. Camera zooms in on the phone's screen. I hold the phone steady. You can tell by the length of the shot on the camera that this is a significant moment. Let the action commence. Now.

LIZ'S DIARY

Wednesday 8th August

Fifth entry

I started today in a black mood but now my mood is bright yellow and green and purple. Because moods do have colours. Yellow is like sunshine – it's a happy colour – and purple is dramatic, and green is . . . something or other.

This is what happened today. I was on the late shift. That meant getting into Coffee Corp at twelve and staying till eight when we close. I slept till ten which was late for me, still clenched with a vice-like anger about the whole Peter thing. Maggie and I hadn't talked about how we both felt. Not properly. *I* didn't want to because she always wins arguments by being so reasonable and forceful and 'I'm your mum so I know better than you' kind of thing. *She* didn't want to because Maggie copes by bottling things up. You have to force her to speak sometimes, and I wasn't going to. We were talking to each other, but we weren't *speaking*. It wasn't like us.

Peter came round yesterday evening, and Maggie told me to come and spend some time with them. We watched TV together. I behaved OK – I suppose it was OK – except the living room didn't feel like our living room. It was a public place with another person there. But it would have been bearable except the cop programme we were watching segued into a steamy sex scene. Suddenly the three of us were watching this couple getting their kit off and falling all over each other.

I couldn't look around. I froze. And I thought – if Maggie gets the remote and changes channel, then she's acknowledged that we all shouldn't be watching this together, which is more embarrassing than us actually watching this together. And Peter certainly couldn't say anything. We all had to pretend that none of us were bothered by all the panting and sighing and moaning. I thought I'd get up and say I needed a drink. Only I didn't because then *they'd* know I was embarrassed.

I wondered what Peter was thinking. Did he like watching this kind of thing? Don't all men? The female actress let out a high-pitched moan and I stared so hard at the carpet my eyes nearly bored holes in it. And then, thankfully, the scene changed and we could all breathe again.

But back to today. When I got to work, there was Sophie behind the bar. I knew Coffee Corp had taken her on, but Jimmy had told me she would be working at the King's Gate branch. But there she was in our shop. Bob was standing with her at the bar explaining something. Jimmy was at the till. When I went back of house to change my shoes and put on my apron, I looked on the duty board and saw next to my name the word 'clearing'. Great. That meant collecting the empties, wiping the tables, seeing to the rubbish. And we were busy too.

By half past three I was shattered. Because there'd been a sudden shower, people had come in off the streets and the tables were almost full. I was tripping over dripping umbrellas. Meanwhile at the bar Sophie was doing her helpless female act and all the time, whatever she was doing, either Jimmy or Bob were standing over her, helping her with the bar, showing her how to mix the happy frappés, explaining stuff. I was surprised at Bob. I would have thought he'd be immune to her charms. Honestly – we'd have been more efficient without her, I thought to myself.

Time to clear the tables. I got the blue plastic tray we use for collecting the empties, the wipes, the spray and donned my plastic gloves. I made my way out to the tables. As I was finishing clearing a table with a half-eaten panini and crumbs from a chocolate muffin, someone said, 'Hi, Liz.'

I recognised the voice. It was Peter. What was he doing here? I looked to see if Maggie was with him but he was alone.

'Oh, hi,' I said.

There I was clutching the tray of empties like a barrier between us. There he was, facing me. My height exactly, his hairy arms covered by the beige jacket he was wearing. The shoulders were darkened by the rain that had damped them. Had he come in on purpose or what?

'I was just passing,' he said, cheerfully.

'Cool,' I said, but my tone of voice expressed the opposite.

'Liz,' he said. 'Can we have a chat? Do you have a break coming up?'

As it happened, I did. I was overdue for my thirty minutes.

In just a few moments Peter and I were sitting down together at a table by the window.

My mind was racing. I wondered what this could be about. Was he trying to suck up to me? Had Maggie sent him? I flexed my fingers, which is a nervous habit I have. I thought I'd better take the initiative here.

'Why are—' I started.

'Liz—' he said, at exactly the same time.

We tried again.

'What do—' I said.

'I want to—'

We both laughed. We had no choice. But it was Peter who took control.

'Liz – Maggie doesn't know I'm here. To tell you the truth, I was passing – I've come in on an impulse. And now I have, I want to say the right thing to you, but – hell – I don't know what that is.'

Half of me sat watching him as if he was a creature from another planet; the other half felt sorry for him.

'It must be pretty uncomfortable for you, being put in the position of deciding whether I should move in or not.'

'No, I'm fine!' I protested.

'Come on!' He grinned at me. 'The truth – all of a sudden this strange bloke might be moving into your house, and you're supposed to get on with him without even knowing him. And you don't feel weird about that?'

'Yeah – I suppose.'

'I just want you to know – I'm aware of that. I know this is difficult for you. But I want you to know I'm never going to take Maggie away from you. I couldn't. She talks about you all the time. She's so proud of you.'

I felt myself redden. I wanted the earth to swallow me, but at the same time I wasn't exactly unhappy.

'I know you need time to get used to this situation. And also, Liz – I want you to know I care about your mum. I'm not just messing around with her.'

I'd been warming to him until he said that. I just didn't want to have him emoting all over me. But I guess he was trying to assure me he wasn't taking her for a ride. And also he was telling me the truth, and I appreciated that. So I thought I'd try telling the truth too.

'You're younger than her,' I stated.

'Yeah. Eight years younger. But it doesn't seem to matter. I'm quite mature for my years.' He laughed.

'I'm finding this whole thing hard to get used to,' I said. 'But I reckon it can't be easy for you either. Because I guess you're worried about what I think of you.'

Our eyes met and I knew I was right.

And that was the moment I began to get used to Peter. Notice I said, 'began'. I appreciated the fact he'd come to talk to me and I liked what he had to say about Mum. I suppose I'd put myself in his shoes for a bit.

'Liz – take your time about this. I don't want you to feel there's any pressure on you.'

'But the lease on your flat . . .' I faltered.

'It won't expire until mid-September. There's no hurry. And by then the situation at work will be clearer.'

'How?' I was curious.

85

Peter made a gesture, zipping up his mouth, as if he wasn't allowed to speak. Maggie had already told me that a lot of his work was investigative, and that there were areas of confidentiality. Only that phoney gesture, that zipping up his mouth, irritated me. I decided to push him.

'Why?' I persisted. 'What are you doing at work that's so important that you can't say? Does Maggie know what you're up to?'

I could see him weighing up the situation. He bit his lip. Then spoke.

'Yes, in part. And there's no reason why you shouldn't know either. You're not a kid.'

I said nothing, but showed I was listening.

'Presumably you've been reading about the by-election in Belton.'

'Didn't the MP die a few weeks ago? And isn't that the place where there was a demonstration and a couple of kids were hurt.'

Peter nodded. I wished I could remember more about what I'd read in the papers. Then I did.

'Hold on – weren't they saying the kids were attacked by a gang of Asians? But I don't believe that report. I reckon it was the Neo-Nazi candidate stirring things up.'

'Do you?' Peter asked, raising his eyebrows.

'Yeah – I mean, no one's been arrested, so even the police can't be sure who did it.'

'What evidence do you have that it *wasn't* how it was reported.'

He threw me a challenging look. I was taken aback. I'd

assumed Peter thought like me and Maggie on these issues. How on earth could she be going out with someone who didn't? For a moment or two I was baffled. Then a slow smile spread over his face.

'We need evidence,' he said softly. Then raised his voice. 'And you might need something to eat before you start work. Can I get you a sandwich? A cake?'

'No,' I grinned at him. 'You get back to work. Right now.'

He winked at me, rose, and left Coffee Corp. I stayed at the table a few minutes longer. I'd understood exactly what he was telling me. He was involved in an investigation to nail the racist element in Belton. I wondered what that would entail? And how dangerous would it be?

I was on his side – how could anyone not be? But then, it wasn't that I objected to him as a bloke, it was more that he was becoming part of our lives whether I liked it or not. But maybe I did like it. Or did I? And what did I want to happen now?

I didn't want him and Maggie to split up. But neither did I exactly want him to move into my house. Heck – I didn't know *what* I wanted. I almost wished someone else would decide for me.

Later, behind the bar, I said to Bob, 'That was my mum's boyfriend. He might be moving in with us.' The words felt OK in my mouth. 'He's a journalist,' I added.

Sophie was at the till and overheard me.

'Your mum's boyfriend? Did he come in specially to see you? How sweet! He's cute.'

Puh-lease!

'So he's a journalist. Is he rich? Jimmy's real dad is loaded!'

Jimmy's real dad? He'd never mentioned anything about that to me. I knew he lived with his mum and step-dad but I never knew he had any contact with his real dad. I wanted to know more but I didn't care to ask Sophie. And how come she knew and I didn't? Well, I suppose they are going out together. But, still.

'Jimmy's going to visit him at his flat – in Park Point! Hello! What would you like? Sorry, can you repeat that? A double espresso and two strawberry happy frappés?'

I waited until the end of the day to speak to Jimmy. Meanwhile, I was doing my Sherlock Holmes act. Thinking it all through. Did this have anything to do with the strop Jimmy was in when I saw him on the bench in Exchange Square the other day? Had his real dad turned up out of the blue? If so, he'd kept it quiet, and that wasn't like Jimmy. I'd have expected him to joke and show off about it. For the rest of the day I observed him. There was something slightly guarded about him. He wasn't fooling about as much as usual. He wasn't joking with the customers. I watched him with Sophie too. I caught him looking at her once or twice, and he seemed almost nervous of her, not like they were intimate or anything. I got the feeling they still weren't totally at ease with each other. Or maybe that was wishful thinking.

Me, Jimmy and Bob were closing down. Bob had left the café to see to the outside seating. That left me and Jimmy turning off machines and throwing out the food we hadn't managed to sell. I liked that, just being alone with him doing normal, everyday things. I was emptying the display cabinet while he brought me over a refuse bag.

'What's this about your real dad?' I asked Jimmy.

He stopped stock-still. Rigid.

'Did Sophie tell you?' he asked after a moment.

I nodded. 'What's it about, Jimmy?'

He cast his eyes around the café nervously. He explained how his real dad had been following him, made himself known to him, and how he found out his mother had lied to him about his past. Imagine! And that he'd seen his dad since then, and he was going to visit him in a couple of days. Heavy stuff.

'Why didn't you tell me this before?' I asked.

He shrugged, and handed me the rubbish bag. I wasn't going to fill it with the uneaten sandwiches just yet.

'You must be feeling so messed up!' I said.

'Yeah – it's all a bit mad.'

'Do you like him?'

'Yeah. He's cool.'

I bit my lip. I hadn't realised before how much you can hide when you talk street talk. Jimmy said his dad was 'cool'. What did that mean? He was telling me nothing – maybe even telling himself nothing.

'Hey, listen, Jimmy, I'm kind of in your situation. Not that I have a new dad or anything – no way! But Maggie's boyfriend might be moving in. Did you see him come in before? So I have a new man in my life, too!'

I told him this because I thought it would help him,

finding he knew someone in a similar situation. Me and my friends do this all the time – we compare our experiences, do the empathy thing. Only Jimmy didn't pick up on this. He just muttered something about that being nice, and he began to lift the sandwiches from the display cabinet and put them in the bag. I carried on. I don't know why. I can be a stubborn bugger at times.

'Has Sophie met your dad?'

'No.'

'It must be hard for you – you'll be learning all over again who you really are.'

I could tell he was listening to me. It was the way that he *wasn't* looking at me that gave it away.

'Look, Jimmy – I know we wind each other up all the time and that, but if you want to talk about it, just say.'

'Like I told you, Liz, I'm cool with it. Sorted.'

I was hurt, the way he dismissed me. It felt like a rejection – a rejection that converted itself into a sudden stab of jealousy. So I said, 'Have you spoken to Sophie about your feelings?'

He looked at me oddly then. 'No.'

I felt better. I wanted to lighten up the whole situation. I said to him, 'Do you know that poem? The Larkin one, about how your parents mess you up? Only it's ruder than that.'

Jimmy grinned – he obviously did know the poem I meant. His eyes alight with mischief, he looked like himself again.

'Remind me,' he said.

I spoke the whole poem aloud, complete with four-letter-word.

'Nice one,' he said. 'All too true.'

I thought to myself, I bet Sophie wouldn't quote poetry at him. Maybe the latest Britney Spears lyric, if he was lucky. But seriously, just for one moment, we connected. Because both of us were going through it with our parents.

Bob came back then and told us to get a move on, and didn't we have homes to go to?

'Remember what I said,' I told Jimmy.

And he said, 'I will.'

So – yellow for sunshine because I've decided that Peter might not turn out to be a bad thing; purple for the drama of Jimmy discovering his real dad; green – come on, Liz – you said when you started this diary you would be honest and write things that might be painful and embarrassing – green . . . for jealousy.

But hold on – I am *not* jealous of Sophie in that I'd plot to separate them or anything like that. No way. Not at all. It's more that I want to be Jimmy's confidante – I want to be the person he talks to about all of this. I'm interested in his situation, and my guess is that Jimmy hides from his true feelings and that's not always a good thing to do. If it was me – if I was in his position – I'd be telling everyone, and analysing how I felt, and everything. But boys don't – do they? Sometimes I think they're more emotional than girls, but they don't think it's manly to show their emotions, so they deflect them – like, they get all worked up over a game of football, or dead excited when they've got hold of some item they're collecting – but when it comes to dealing with people, they shove those feelings down.

No, I'll never understand boys. I also don't understand what Jimmy sees in Sophie. Well, apart from the obvious things. But there's depth in him, despite all his fooling around. He has depth and style, and frankly she is just an airhead. If I was going out with Jimmy, we'd have a *real* relationship – we'd talk, we'd sit quietly sometimes not saying anything, we'd learn about each other – it wouldn't just be dates at the movies and texting . . .

But it will never happen. And now I've had fun imagining it, I can just let it go. Jimmy will be the best boyfriend I never had. And that's final.

JIMMY

Cut from the opening credits to Jimmy Keane on a train into the city. He's sitting at a window seat, chin propped on his hands, lost in thought. The soundtrack is something from Coldplay. Cut from Jimmy to what he sees from the window – groups of red-bricked, slate-roofed houses, untidy back gardens, playpools, washing. Back to Jimmy – deep focus on half-empty carriage. Jimmy in black vest top, torn jeans, Reeboks. Zoom into his face. Voice-over commences:

'Most kids are brought up by their dads. Most kids hang out with their dads. Not me. My dad arrived in my life less than three weeks ago. I'm on my way to his flat right now.'

That's good. Now I think I need a flashback. Yeah, because I want to mess around with the time frame here. Because – right – my past's collided with my present, so it feels like I should zigzag between them. We need a special effect now – a blackout – or the sound of a rewind button:

Crackle. Buzz. Psssssss.

This scene takes place last week, when I'm meeting Mike for the second time. I'm walking into the hotel lobby where he said he'd find me.

The lobby is huge. Cream pillars, heavy chandeliers

93

dripping with glass hanging from the ceiling. To my right is a bank of desks manned by an army of uniformed receptionist and concierges. To my left, a mezzanine floor with tables and chairs laid out for afternoon teas. There's even a bloke in a dinner suit tinkling at a piano. In my head I'm going, 'Of all the bars, in all the world—'

'Jimmy.'

Mike – my dad – is coming towards me, dressed in a beige suit teamed with a chocolate shirt. His smile is open and friendly. My dad. My real dad.

Crackle. Buzz. Psssss.

Here's a flashback in a flashback. A few days before that, me, mum and Steve sitting round the kitchen table. It's big debate time. Don't you hate the way parents do this? Sit you down to have a talk? Making a big deal out of stuff? They look hassled, Mum and Steve. Mum's not been sleeping. I can see pouches under her eyes. She hasn't bothered to wash her hair. Steve is quiet, serious. Mum goes:

'Jimmy – I know I don't have the right to stop you seeing him. But can I give you my version of what happened?'

I don't need to listen to this. I don't want Mum making up my mind for me. Only I'm trapped here. I can't get out.

'I know you want to tell me,' I say.

She nods. Steve reaches out and takes her hand. Two of them. One of me.

'I was only nineteen when I met him and I got carried away by his determination to marry me. I thought it was romantic. But Mike turned out to be a bully. He wanted me under his thumb all the time, and when I kicked against it, he had his way of making me do what he wanted. Once or twice he was violent—'

'What? Did he beat you up?'

'Well, no, but—'

'He didn't beat you up. OK. Got it.'

'Jimmy – it was more subtle than that. I realised he wasn't a good man to be married to. When I disentangled myself, I took you where he couldn't find us. I thought it would be better for you not to know about him. I wanted to distance myself from the mistake I made. Maybe I was wrong, I don't know. I wanted a fresh start. Also – I didn't think he would be a good father.'

'Did he ever mistreat me?'

'No, but—'

'So you just thought he would be a bad father, and you took me away.'

'I had my reasons.'

'Listen to her,' Steve said.

They were making me angry, the way they were ganging up on me, pretending to give me freedom of choice but taking it away at the same time.

'I'm gonna find out for myself, OK?' I scowled at them.

On second thought, we'll delete that scene. Snip. It falls onto the cutting room floor. It never happened.

Fast forward. Me on the train again. We're getting closer to the city now. Tower blocks are looming in the distance. I like the clacking of the wheels on the track. I have to admit I'm a little bit nervous. Not of Mike, but the whole Park Point thing. These apartments are seriously posh. One or two of the local soap stars live there. But then, Mike isn't short of a bob or two.

Crackle. Buzzzzz.

Back to the hotel scene. He meets me in the lobby, and leads me up to the mezzanine where we order tea. We sit at a round table with a snowy white tablecloth, napkins and silver cutlery. A waitress in black wearing a white apron comes to take our order. Pretty cool, this – someone making me coffee for a change. Soon we're tucking into scones and cakes. Mike explains how he's in the process of starting up his own security company. He asks me about my job. I explain the Coffee Corp thing is only part time, and how I'm at college really.

'So you must be short of funds,' he says, smiling.

'You could say that.'

From his wallet he takes four – yeah, *four* – fifty pound notes. 'This will tide you over,' he says.

I do try to refuse, I really do. But he insists. He puts his wallet back in his jacket and there's an end of it.

'Carol will go ballistic,' I say.

'She needn't know,' Mike says. 'And if I can't give money to my own son, who can I give it to? I've more than enough for my own needs. And all these years, I haven't been able to support you. Let me do something for you now.'

I put the notes in my jeans pocket and I can't help planning how I'm going to cancel the debt with Amir, get some decent gear, the *Star Wars* collection and maybe also that Stanley Kubrick boxed set. Or maybe even that camcorder

I've been dreaming of. But also I'm listening to him. He's talking about the past again.

'There were things I did which I regret. I admit that. But Jimmy, what I want you to understand is that people change. I want to make something of my life now. I want to settle down. Judge me by my actions now.'

I glance at his face, see those feathery scars and notice also how he has two indentations on the sides of his nose, and as he breathes they go in and out. I find myself studying his features and seeing myself embedded in him. The camera would switch between us now, picking up our similarities. I tell Mike about the AS results due soon, and my interest in film. He's very encouraging, very interested. He says he likes the Bond movies.

'Nice one, Mike!' I say.

He says, 'Can you try to call me Dad?'

'Yeah,' I say. 'Dad.' He reaches out and squeezes my hand. Holds it tight for a moment. Then lets go.

Fast forward.

A new scene. Me and Sophie round at her place with no one else in the house. We're watching a DVD and I'm kissing her. Giving her the full JK seduction treatment but not getting anywhere. She wipes her mouth after we break away for a moment. I'm scared to talk about this – the way she's keeping me at a distance. Doesn't she like me enough? I'm not sure what to do, where to take it from here. I'm not going to start groping her unless I get some kind of green light. I'm getting desperate – and horny.

'Tell you what,' I say, softly. 'I'll take you out for a meal tomorrow night – anywhere you want to go.'

'Yeah, right,' she says. 'Maccy D's?'

'No. Anywhere,' I say. 'As in anywhere. You name the place. I'm in funds.'

She's still for a moment and looks at me like I'm winding her up.

'Did I tell you?' I say, happy to break my resolution to keep the whole Mike thing quiet. 'I've met my real dad. He's just given me two hundred quid. And that's for starters.'

She's interested. I tell her a version of the Mike story. She says that's so exciting. So I fall on her again and this time I get inside her bra. Then the phone rings and it's her mum warning her they're on their way back. She puts her hand on my dick over my jeans and laughs. Then says she'd better make herself look straight for her parents.

Every movie needs a sex scene, only I'm not sure this is it. I edit it out. Maybe later on I'll go for something really hot. We'll see.

Fast forward.

I'm in the city now and on my way to Park Point. I hear the clunk and roar of cranes and turn to see a building in the process of being demolished. Like everyone, I stop for a while and have a look. The diggers, like mechanical serpents, nibble jerkily at the entrails of the building's corpse – a spew of grey, dusty wires that held the concrete together. I can see interior walls exposed to the sky, halves of rooms, the outline of a staircase. Still the diggers eat away, and another rush of concrete rubble falls to the ground. This is definitely going in the movie. I'm waiting in case something dramatic happens, like the whole building collapses, but the destruction is a slow, piecemeal process. Eventually I get bored and walk away.

Park Point isn't one of those all glass and metal tower blocks of apartments that are springing up everywhere. It's more exclusive than that, a squat, rectangular building that used to be a warehouse, or maybe a sixties office block. The red bricks have been cleaned and there's a fringe of gardens around it. I have to use an entryphone to get in. Mike's – my dad's – voice comes back at me instantly. I hear a click, and push open the door. He's told me to use the stairs to get to the first floor.

I walk into an atrium. I think that's what they call it – it's an oblong, interior open space. There are doors to the apartments on each long side of the oblong. In the middle is a Japanese-inspired internal garden with areas of pebbles, a fountain and concrete balls arranged artistically in various places. Cool. There are three more floors above and each has a gallery running along its side giving access to the doors. Above me walkways criss-cross from one gallery to the other. I look up at the galleries and the whole building reminds me of something, somewhere I've seen before in a movie or on TV. It's those galleries, with the lines of doors above me on either side.

A door opens just in front of me, and there's Mike. I leave the atrium and walk in. It's all pale wood and wooden laminate flooring. He leads me through a corridor and I glimpse a luxury bathroom to my left complete with power shower and a Jacuzzi-style bath. We're in the living area now. Wicked. Cream carpet, white leather settee, huge plasma telly. One side of the room has an extension, a sort of conservatory, with a tiled floor and a couple of loungers. The view gives on to the street and the bar opposite. I am seriously impressed.

Mike says it's the best he could get – he's only renting, until things settle down here for him. I'm not really listening. I'm busy taking it all in. I notice the kitchen now, to one side, all gleaming metal and white. Spotless. I realise some music is playing. I frown while I try to place it. Early Mick Jagger. 'Wild Horses'.

Dad's fussing now, asking would I like anything to drink, to eat? He offers coffee, tea, something stronger? We settle on bottles of lager from the tall fridge in the kitchen. He opens a packet of Kettle crisps, throws them into a bowl, and we sit on either end of the settee, half facing each other. I take a slug from my bottle. I can't believe all this is happening to me.

I tell my dad how much I like it here and a smile spreads over his face. He's wearing a cream T-shirt with three buttons at the neck – the top is undone. His jeans are neat and new. He springs up again and offers to show me the rest of the apartment. We go back into the corridor and he opens a door by the bathroom. It's his bedroom. There's just a double bed in it with a navy throw over the top. There are white walls, fitted wardrobes, and one chair. Next to that room is another, smaller one. It's a second bedroom with a single bed. The mattress is bare. Neither room has any proper windows.

Instead, close to the top, there's an oblong of Perspex that gives onto the atrium.

Back in the lounge now and already we've both finished our lager. Dad gets some more. He's clearly a bit awkward, having me round. I'm not used to having adults nervous around me.

We talk about the flat a while and he asks me about where I live. I tell him it's an old, rambling house, and Steve's always doing things to it as bits keep falling off or going wrong. Dad says that's the problem with old houses. We drink some more. Then he asks me whether Carol knows I'm here. I say that she does and he looks surprised. I tell him how she's warned me to be careful, but it bugs me, the way she thinks I can't look after myself. Mike nods thoughtfully at that.

He asks how things are. I find I'm getting chatty now – the lager? Whatever. I tell him about Sophie, how she got a job at Coffee Corp because she's really into me and that. Dad says I must bring her round – he'd like to meet her. He asks if it's serious and I tell him that it's early days. I mention that she's away on holiday, but she'll be back before the AS results. He asks me how I expect to do, and I tell him it's a lottery. When you walk away from an exam, it's impossible to work out how you've done. I explained to him about the module system, and how you can always retake.

Sitting here, shooting the crap, I feel really good. In this wicked apartment, just me and my dad, thinking it through, straight talking. I like the person I'm becoming. I start talking about film again. I explain why Tarantino is one of my favourite directors and all about the Manga comic influence in *Kill Bill*. Mike's really interested and asks me questions. He says, isn't Tarantino a bit violent, and I'm like, it's cartoon violence. You're not supposed to take it seriously. I tell him Hitchcock is much more disturbing. We agree and talk about *The Birds*, which he's seen.

Two blokes, shooting the crap about movies.

When the Kettle crisps have gone, he goes and gets some more. We're both relaxing now. I kick off my trainers and spread myself out. He asks me about life at home and how I get on with Steve and the kids. He's not fishing or anything – it's more that he's totally interested in me. I've never had this before, someone hanging on my every word. I suppose if you have normal parents you get used to this, I don't know. But I'm not used to it and it feels good. I say Steve's a bit of a wimp, under Mum's thumb. I feel a bit bad about saying it but it's kind of true. He's docile, likes the quiet life. The kids are just kids, I tell him. Stacey's a bit of a goody-goody, Kyle's just mad.

Dad says, if they get too much for you, you can always come and bed down here.

People say that kind of thing but they never really mean it. I imagine most nights my dad would have mates round, and he wouldn't want me. I tell him that because by now my tongue is loose – too much lager – good quality stuff – and I say whatever's on my mind.

Dad says he doesn't know too many people yet, then he goes into the kitchen bit of the flat and opens a drawer. Gets out a keyring with a couple of keys on it and brings it over.

'This is for you,' he says. 'I want you to treat this place as your own. Come and stay any time. Bring your girlfriend. I'll get the bed made up for you.'

'What?' I say, a bit dense, befuddled. 'I can stay here?'

'You don't even have to ring,' Dad says. 'You're my son, after all. If I'd stayed with Carol, you'd be living with me.'

I accept the keys. I half listen while he explains about how to get in through the front. Then – get this – he hands me another hundred quid, laughs, and says it's pocket money.

This time, I try to refuse. I tell him I don't want to be taking all his money. He laughs again and thrusts the notes in my jeans pocket and for a moment I think he's going to mock-wrestle me, and I tense myself. But he doesn't. He sits back again and asks me, 'How am I doing?'

'What do you mean?'

'How am I doing as a dad? I've had no experience up till now. I'm feeling my way. What do you want from me, Jimmy? Just say.'

I'm lost for words now. You never really think about what you want from your parents. But right now he seems pretty perfect to me – I imagine what my mates would think, seeing me here, in this awesome flat, with the empty bottles and that.

I tell him, 'You just carry on what you're doing.'

He beams at me again. Then he goes to the bathroom. I'm alone, and I can't quite believe all this is happening. I'm really beginning to rate my dad. Not because of all the money, not even because of this apartment. (Sophie will like it. I'm going to be in there.) No – I like my dad because he listens to me – because he's got time for me – he's putting me in the centre. I hear the flush from the bathroom. He's back now. I smile at him to show him how much I'm enjoying this afternoon.

I ask him to tell me about himself. He gives a dismissive laugh. But he talks anyway. I learn about my grandparents – my granddad was an engineer in the mills and my grandma worked in a café. He was an only child and my granddad died when he was twelve, but he says he didn't mind too much. His dad used to whip him whenever his mum said he was out of order. He didn't like school much because he failed his eleven plus and went to the local secondary modern where all the teachers treated you like muck. He says after his dad died, he became a bit rebellious, hard to handle. He was in with a gang of lads who used to get into trouble. Then he tells me how it was Carol who saved him from all that.

He comes to a halt then. He says it's not for him to talk about those days. Maybe he will eventually. But he says that the best thing to come out of that marriage was me. He tells me how much he likes the way I've turned out – that I seem confident and mature, much more sorted than he was at my age. Then he tells me he had an uncle who used to paint, and his pictures were exhibited in the local gallery. Did I think my talent for movie-making might be inherited?

And more stuff like that. Then I remember I said I'd meet Amir in town. He asks me about Amir – says is he a Muslim? I said, yeah, I reckoned so, but we'd never talked about it. My dad goes quiet and I reckon it's his Iraq days that made him react like that. One day I'm gonna get him to tell me more about that time.

He tells me again to treat the place as my own and I say I will. At the door we shake hands. His grip is strong and powerful. He squeezes my hand until it almost hurts me. He slaps me on the back. Awkwardly, I punch him in the chest. We grin at each other.

I wander through the atrium and out down the stairs. OK, so I am a bit rat-arsed, and it is still the afternoon. But this is what life is all about – and I'm living it. I feel good and warm and fuzzy. I push off to meet Amir.

LIZ'S DIARY

Thursday 16th August

Sixth entry

Three As and a B! How good is that? Basically this means that I can apply to the uni I want to, and I have a pretty good chance of getting in. One more year left at college and then – the big, wide world. Let me at it!

But I'll go back to the rest of the day – as there are things to tell. I went to college to collect my results in person. I can't really pretend I slept last night, and this morning my stomach was in knots and I kept dropping things. Maggie was dead reassuring and said however I did, she didn't mind. Which I knew was true, and that does help. Some of my mates have parents who they're scared of letting down, if they don't do well enough. What right have parents got to make you dance to their tune? Us kids, we didn't ask to be born. Just because you bring someone up, it doesn't mean you have rights over them. They're not your possessions. This is what I think, anyway.

But back to the day – Maggie couldn't be with me as she had work, but that was OK. Approaching college I had my head down but already I could hear screams and squeals –

I hate that hysteria you get on results day. It was the same at GCSE. The girls are much worse than the boys. They cry if they do badly, cry if they do well, hug each other, jump up and down, then adjust their hair and smile sweetly for the local press who come to take photos.

Without making eye contact with anyone I went to the library where the results slips were, was given mine by one of the deputy principals, opened it, took a moment or two to understand what was written on it, then it sank in. A for English Literature, History and Politics, and B for Psychology, which I was going to drop anyway. My knees trembled. I wanted to tell someone only I didn't want to get sucked into all the hugging and squealing. I wandered outside and sat on a wall, got out my mobile, and rang Maggie. I could tell by her voice how pleased she was.

I should have moved away then. But I was too late. Along came Sophie.

'What did you get?' she asked.

'Three As and a B,' I mumbled. I don't like to show off.

'Well done!' Sophie said, and she looked genuinely pleased for me. 'I always thought you were the clever type.'

I wasn't sure whether to ask her how she'd done, but she told me anyway.

'Two Bs and two Cs,' she said. 'Which is good enough for me. But I'm so glad I've caught you.' She sat down on the wall next to me and wriggled close. 'We haven't seen each other since I came back from holiday.'

This was true. She'd been away for the last week in Majorca. I hadn't missed her.

'I have so much to tell you! And what do you think of my tan?'

I inspected it and told her I thought it suited her.

'I know! I had the best time! The best, best time!' She sighed expressively. I didn't encourage her. I just wanted to get home, ring up some of the family, and get used to my results. But Sophie wasn't having any of that.

'I've so much to tell you. First of all, I'm not going back to Coffee Corp. I'm jacking it in.'

'Why?' I asked.

'I've got a better job working on a jewellery concession in Harvey Nicks. Anyway, it was gross, cleaning out the toilets and collecting empties. But that's not my main news!'

She paused so I would ask her what it was. She was lucky I was in a good mood. I played along with her.

'So tell me.'

Sophie looked around, then leant over and whispered this to me. 'I've had the most amazing holiday romance!'

But she's going out with Jimmy!

'Oh, Liz, I didn't mean it to happen, but you know how these things are. I met him at the club we went to. I thought he was Spanish but he comes from London, actually. His name is Mark. I've got some piccies in my phone I can show you.'

As she fumbled in her jeans pocket, I said, 'What about Jimmy?'

'He doesn't have to know!' she giggled, then flicked through her shots of this smarmy poseur she'd been playing with.

She asked me what I thought, and I said he was OK.

'Are you splitting with Jimmy then?' I asked her.

'Oh, help!' she exclaimed. 'No – I don't think so. But I don't know! I'll have to see how I feel when I meet him again. Honestly, Liz, it's such a relief to be able to tell someone about this. You're such a good listener.'

I changed the subject. 'How were Jimmy's results?'

'I don't know. He's not texted. How is he?'

'OK.'

And then I saw a bunch of the other girls approaching us clutching their results slips and I beat a sharp exit. They descended on Sophie and hugged her and clucked like chickens.

So in between bursts of happiness at my results, I began to worry about Jimmy. Sophie had cheated on him. I knew, and he didn't. So what do I do now? Tell him? Wait for Sophie to decide whether to dump him or not?

And how would it affect him? Maybe not too badly. Since Sophie had gone away he'd been meeting with his dad. His dad even came in once or twice, and I was able to get a good look at him. You could certainly tell he'd been in the army. He stands stiff and straight, and his head's close shaven. There's something controlled and powerful about him. He's not like Jimmy at all. It makes me wonder what's more important in bringing someone up – nature or nurture? Do you grow like your biological parent or like the one who influences you the most?

But one thing's for certain, Jimmy is infatuated with his dad. He keeps talking about him – how he was in Iraq, how he's got all this cash, how his flat is awesome. He's boasting all the time. But the funny thing is, it's not the kind of boasting that gets to me. Sophie's sly digs make me want to hit her; Jimmy just goes on like a kid with a trophy dad. Look what my dad can do – my dad's bigger'n your dad – that kind of thing. I suppose it's because he's never had a dad of his own before. He's regressing to his childhood, going through that stage that kids do when they think their mum and dad can do no wrong. It's cute, in a way.

It's never bothered me, not being brought up with a dad. But then I'm a girl and I reckon it's different for boys. Just as I model myself on Maggie, Jimmy needs to model himself on someone. I just hope this Mike is the right model.

All the way home I worried about Jimmy. I hoped his results were OK – I wouldn't text him in case he didn't want to tell me. His college was the other end of town, and I didn't know anyone who knew him. Also I had to think what to do about Sophie.

I arrived home at the exact same moment as the delivery bloke from the flower shop, who was partly obscured by the huge bouquet he was carrying.

'Miss Elizabeth Burns?' he enquired.

A bit taken aback, I owned up that I was me, and took the flowers. Inside, I opened the little envelope with the card to say who it was from.

'Well done! Brilliant results! Love from Peter.'

I smiled. That was cool of him. But at the same time, just a little intimidating. But today, I can forgive anyone anything. Three As and a B. Three As and a B!!! Because I was on my own, I danced down the hall and into the kitchen. I was crazy with happiness and relief.

JIMMY

As I glance at my results slip I know my grades are going to be shit. Like I've always said, exam results don't bother me. I know when I put my mind to it, I'll be able to get the qualifications. So I don't know why I feel gutted when I work out I've just got one D in Eng Lit and the rest are fails. Like I said, I'm expecting this.

I walk home from college by myself. This is definitely an out-take – I'm not even putting it in the extra scene selection of the DVD of my life, the movie. I'm just a bit shocked at how sick I feel about this. Even though I know I did no work, it's like I'm labelled now – failure. It's not fair. One AS level at grade D. Great. But what was it Clark Gable said? 'Frankly, my dear, I don't give a damn.' Yeah, well, I don't give a damn.

Of course, I'm also thinking about what Mum – and Dad – are going to say. I know they'll both be disappointed. I just don't want them to give me grief about it. I know I've done badly – I don't need telling. I'm pounding the streets locked up in my own black mood, and it's getting blacker by the minute. I reckon I just need to be alone for a while. Then I'll be OK.

But it's a day of bad luck, and the next thing that happens

is that I hear the sound of a car hooter beeping furiously, an engine slowing down, and it's my mum. She throws open the door.

'Have you got them?'

I slide into the front seat and try out a non-committal, 'Yeah.'

We're parked outside someone's house. They've turned their front garden into a parking area for two cars. One of them is there now – a blue Fiat Seicento. Funny how Italian cars have innate style, even the cheapest. I've always fancied myself in an Alfa Romeo, but if I was creating a road movie, I might even choose a huge, clapped out old Fiat.

'Jimmy,' my mum goes. 'You're not saying anything.'

This is an accurate observation. I'm hoping she might be able to read my results slip by telepathy to spare me the full-on horror of having to tell her. I examine the shelf in front of me and see Kyle's reading book from school, one black woollen glove and several crumpled tissues.

'So they weren't good?' Mum persists.

'One D,' I mumble. 'Failed the rest.'

I can't do justice to the silence that follows. It's even a visual silence. Nothing stirs in the car, in the street. My throat tightens, my stomach stops digesting food, even my heart is still. I'm waiting.

Life begins again as Mum lets out a deep breath. I'm thinking, maybe this isn't going to be too bad. She just repeats:

'One D – after a whole year at college.'

'I know,' I say. 'I'll retake next year.'

Suddenly the car engine starts with a roar. Mum moves

savagely into first and we're off. We swerve round corners, pull up with a jolt at traffic lights. Finally we get home.

'I'm sorry, OK?' I tell her.

'It's yourself you ought to be saying sorry to.'

Here we go again. Straight into lecture mode. Coming out with all that daft parent-speak. All smugged up with self-righteousness.

She storms into the house and I follow her. Everyone's there. The kids are off school and Steve's given himself a week's holiday to look after them. There's a friend of Stacey's there too, a demure little Jamaican girl with her hair in corn rows. She's wearing a pink Barbie top.

Carol storms into the front room.

'One D, the rest fails,' she announces to Steve and the assembled kids.

My shame is now public. Cheers, Mum.

'Not good,' Steve concurs, but does shoot me a sympathetic glance.

I decide to shout now, just to frighten them all off.

'Look – I'm going to retake. OK? I'll go into college tomorrow and see someone, before I go in to work.'

So much fuss about some stupid exams.

'Jimmy,' my mum goes. 'What I'm going to say is for your own good. Retaking's going to get you nowhere unless you start working. All last year you just sat on your backside. It's not just a matter of resitting, but of making some resolutions about spending your time differently. It's about attitude, Jimmy.'

I really need this right now. Talk about getting the boot in.

'Mummy?' says Stacey. 'Has Jimmy done badly in his exams?'

'Yes, he has,' Mum spits. 'And it's his own fault.'

'Carol,' Steve says warningly. I glance at him. Usually he never says anything much. But I can see he looks alarmed at my mum. For some reason, she's completely lost it.

'What I can't bear to see,' she continues, 'is you throwing your life away. You've got talent, Jimmy, but all you ever do is fool around, make the least possible effort, you only do what appeals to you, you've got no sense of responsibility. Whatever's easiest, you do. And I know I'm being harsh and I know I'll regret saying all of this later, but if I don't, then no one else will. Get real, Jimmy. You messed up – now put yourself straight.'

Who the hell does she think she is? I hit back as I'm cornered. This is like *Fight Club* – bare-knuckle combat, Steve as the referee, the kids as audience. The thought gives me courage. So I aim below the belt.

'I messed up? What about you? You weren't so perfect when you were my age.'

I shudder from the recoil. It was cruel, I know. But I'm looking at her and thinking, not only did she walk out on my dad, but she hid his existence from me. And all I did is fail some stupid exams. Who's the villain here? I see my blow reached its target. She's white with anger. Steve puts his hand on her arm.

'How dare you!' she spits. Then I see her face begin to sag. The anger's replaced by something else. 'Look, Jimmy. I made one mistake, but after that I did my level best to do right by you. I gave you everything I could. Till Steve came along, I've been both mother and father to you. I worked every hour God sent so we could have a roof over our heads. You have no right to accuse me.'

'Mummy works very hard,' Stacey said. 'Not like you, Jimmy.'

Her Barbie friend was watching us, sucking her thumb. I'm beginning to feel like everyone's got it in for me.

'Just lay off me, all of you!' I shout. It was a stupid move. I was sounding desperate. Mum takes advantage of my weakness and moves in for the kill.

'We'll leave the past out of this. I'm only interested in your future, Jimmy. Believe it or not, I love you. I want you to have the best life has to offer. This is what this whole argument is about. I just need to see you're serious about college.'

'All you ever do is criticise me,' I jab back.

'For your own good.'

'My dad never criticises me.'

I hoped it would be the knock-out blow. It certainly silenced her. Ten – nine – eight. But she's up again.

'He doesn't know you like I do.'

'You never gave him the opportunity,' I tell her.

I'm winning on points.

She says, 'Jimmy, there's a lot you don't know about what happened. Just don't meddle. We're talking about your AS results.'

'Fuck my AS results,' I say. Screams from the kids. Steve warns, 'Watch it!' Mum is now flaming with anger. The bad word was a wrong move.

116

'Jimmy – you've changed since he's come into your life. You'd have never sworn like that before. He's not doing you any good.'

'That's where you're wrong. *Your* language is worse than his. My dad is OK – you've misjudged him.'

'Don't make my mistake.'

'What – in getting rid of him? No danger of that. I'm sticking by him.'

'Stick by him, then! Go to him, why don't you! Go and tell HIM about your results! Let him try to sort you out! I wash my hands of you!'

She's lost it completely. She's heaving with sobs now and, to say the truth, I'm a bit scared. Stacey is sobbing and her friend joins in in sympathy. Steve's arm's round Mum. I'm the big villain here.

I shout, 'All right, then, I'm going.'

'She didn't mean it,' Steve says.

But if my mum can act the big drama queen, so can I. How does she think I feel? She's virtually turned me out of my home.

'I'm going,' I say.

I storm upstairs and throw some clothes, some overnight things, in my sports bag. I don't really know why I'm doing this. I just want to score points – I want to make Mum sorry – and I want her to apologise to me – I want to be somewhere where I'm not made to feel like the world's biggest loser. I want to be with my dad. I need his unconditional admiration. I can't be doing with Mum's constant carping and hysterical outbursts.

I'm only going to pretend to move out, I tell myself. Just give them all a shock.

I run down the stairs from my attic bedroom, and hear Stacey and her friend still crying.

'I'm going!' I shout, and slam the door.

So here I am, out in the street, late afternoon, with my sports bag and my dad's key in my pocket.

Am I leaving home? Probably. I don't know. I'll see.

I notice I'm trembling with – some emotion – don't know which one. The things Mum said are coming back at me like a sniper's bullets – *it's your own fault, you've got no sense of responsibility, you messed up.* She was totally out of order. Totally out of order. And *she* told *me* to go to Mike – so, OK, then – I will.

I don't really know where my feet are taking me. Soon I find myself at the train station. Going into the city seems a good move as I want to get as far away as possible from that place formerly known as home. I don't really notice the other people on the platform, don't even take any interest in what train I get on. I'm still too churned up to start thinking straight. The way my mum laid into me – like I was some sort of criminal – and then saying she loved me – and I'm supposed to believe that?

I reach the main line interchange in the city and wander off. Now I'm thinking, I'll go to my dad's. And a thought strikes me. What if he also goes nuts about my results? Maybe all parents are like that – what was that poem Liz quoted at me? I reckon you can't trust anyone that you're related to. They all expect too much from you. Yeah, I'm alone here, walking into the city like one of those characters in the Westerns – Clint Eastwood – John Wayne? I'm alone, I have no history. No – my history is a mystery. It rhymes. Nice one. I'm striding into the city on a mission. What mission?

I don't know. I'm just walking aimlessly. I cross through the business part of the city, past Chinatown, towards the university where all the bars, restaurants and cinemas are. Alone. You know, if I ended up on the streets tonight no one would care. And if I did it would serve them right.

Automatically I walk into the foyer of the Ritz cinema, a trad old-fashioned movie house that has been here as long as I remember. They only have eight screens and big reductions for students. I scan the digital display advertising the current programme and my eyes light on a futuristic cop thriller which has had good reviews and was supposed to have ace special effects. I buy a ticket, some popcorn and make my way to Screen Five.

I post the popcorn into my mouth and resist the ads telling me to visit Scotland for my holidays and to drink a certain sort of exclusive lager. I'm whizzed through the action-packed mini-previews of coming attractions. The censor's certificate flashes up, and next thing, I'm seated by some masked gunman in a jeep speeding along a mountain pass chasing an all-black sports car – and I'm busy working out what's happening, who's who, noticing the swift editing and feeling dizzy with it, deafened by the over-loud speakers in the auditorium, loving the feeling of being cocooned, then thrown about by the movie. Squealing car brakes. A collapsing building. A blonde swimming sinuously underwater.

Don't ask me what the film's about. I don't know and don't care. I'm in the movie, in it, not here sitting on a crummy old velvet cinema seat. I'm dazed and confused by the action, not thinking, just seeing. And it flashes in my mind then that the cinema is a kind of drug to me. It blots stuff out. It takes me to another reality. A better one, to tell you the truth. One where stuff works out OK in the end – well, most of the time at any rate. I'm feeling better, and enjoy the final sequence where just about everyone is out to get the good guy. The similarity with my situation is not lost on me.

It's over, and reluctantly I get up and walk out of the auditorium through that transitional tunnel to the foyer, the street and real life. I turn my phone back on and there's a queue of messages. Mates from college, Amir, my mum. My mum again. And my mum again. Sorry. I'm not in the mood.

The phone says it's quarter to eight. I'm not sure what to do now. I quite like this feeling of being cut adrift. Only I'm hungry, and I have nowhere to sleep tonight. I'm thinking, I could turn up at my dad's and say I haven't got my results yet – they're being posted to me. I just don't want to risk him being disappointed in me at this stage. I don't want to see Sophie now either. I think about texting Amir – he went through all this results crap two years ago. But first I decide to get some nosh – some fries, maybe. I head back into the centre of the city, and there, coming towards me, is Liz.

120

She looks really shocked to see me. Do I look that bad? I say, hey. She's on her own.

'I'm meeting some friends,' she explains. 'We're going out for a drink.'

Now get this. I am really pleased to see Liz. Don't ask me why, but she is in fact the person I want to be with right now. She doesn't look half bad, either. Black leather jacket which I've not seen on her before, torn denims, and her hair is messy but sleek. Her eye make-up suits her.

'Cool,' I say.

'Where are you off to?' she asks me.

'I'm running away from home,' I mug, swinging my sports bag nonchalantly.

She laughs at me. 'Poor little orphan Jimmy.'

'Nobody loves me!'

She looks at me in a funny way then. She says, 'What about Sophie?'

'I should text her, I suppose. Whatever.' I make a bid for Liz's company then. 'You got time for a drink before your drink, if you get my meaning?'

She *is* looking at me in a funny way. She's one of those girls who has X-ray vision. She stares straight through you. I know she knows something is wrong. I like/don't like this.

'Let's walk around a while,' she says. 'I don't have to be on time or anything.'

We fall into step with each other and head north.

'Jimmy,' she says. 'Let's cut the crap. Are you really running away from home?'

'No. I was winding you up. Been to the gym.'

Then this girl grabs my sports bag and unzips it. Sees my spare clothes, my bits and pieces.

'Come on,' she demands. 'The truth.'

Because we're walking side by side and not facing each other I find it's easier to talk. We're walking past the hotel where I met my dad. Top-hatted doormen stand outside seeing to the taxis.

'My results were rubbish, my mum went ballistic and here I am.'

'So you've not heard from Sophie?'

Sophie? Liz seems to be obsessed with Sophie. 'No. And I'm weighing up whether to kip at my dad's. I've got the key.'

We get to a major junction and join the crowd under starter's orders at the traffic lights. The green man flashes and we all start walking.

'What were your results?' Liz asks.

I tell her. She doesn't say anything for a minute. Then, 'Is that what you were expecting?'

'Kind of. I didn't work much. I did revise for the language paper but I got the days mixed up – did the wrong revision. And it didn't help that I'd been cutting lessons. I didn't think it would be as bad as that, though.'

'What are you going to do?' she asks.

'Retake.'

'Why don't you change colleges? Make a new start somewhere else?'

'Could do,' I say, and think that's not a bad idea. She suggests we go down by the canal and we turn left, down a cobbled path. Years ago the canal was most definitely a no-go area, junkie heaven, the polluted water stinking, litter everywhere. Then the city authorities decided on a face-lift, cleaned it, converted the warehouses along its banks to swish apartments, gave a couple of trendy pubs a licence, and now it's a leisure area. But if you walk further along it you can lose so-called civilisation and end up somewhere a little more quiet, and a little more secluded. We did. We found a bench and sat down.

Now normally if I was with a girl down here, I'd be trying it on already. It's that kind of place. Smoochy, romantic. Trees on the banks. The hint of ripples on the water. Only I was with Liz. Who is my mate, and you don't risk messing with your mates. And I have Sophie and I'm not the cheating type, never have been. But glancing at her now, I'm seeing how, with a different script, there could be a whole alternative ending here. But, no. Because, to tell you the truth, Liz scares me. She's scaring me now.

'So, dish. Tell me what happened with your mum.'

'I couldn't get it past the censors.'

'Jimmy!'

'Forget it. How were your results?'

'OK. I'm waiting to hear about your mum.'

So I told her.

LIZ'S DIARY

Thursday, 17th August, continued

Seventh entry

'She certainly overreacted,' I told him. I was watching Jimmy carefully and saw how pleased he was when I said that. It always feels good when someone sticks up for you. So I carried on.

'You were probably already feeling pretty bad, and she put the boot in.'

'You're too right,' Jimmy said. I noticed he was joggling his knees. He was discomposed, reliving all his anger.

'And even if she thought you hadn't been working hard enough, she needn't have told you then.'

He was still for a moment. Then he said, 'I did do *some* work.'

I laughed at him and dug him in the ribs. 'Ow, Liz!' he exclaimed. 'You hurt!'

'But by the sound of it,' I carried on, 'I reckon this argument was about something else. Parents do that, don't they? They're angry about one thing, but they have a go at you for another. Do you know – what I think this was really about, was your dad.'

'How do you make that out?' he asked me.

'Well, she feels she's losing control of you. So by ranting and shouting at you, it's her way of regaining control. Not a very sensible way, but she was going with her emotions. She's probably hurt by you being so interested in your dad, so she wants to hurt you back. When she thinks about it, she'll hate herself for what she's done.'

Jimmy was quiet for a long time after I said that. It gave me time to wonder what the hell I was doing there with Jimmy by the canal when forty-five minutes ago I should have been in the bar with my mates knocking back vodka shots to celebrate my AS results.

'My mum's been texting me,' Jimmy said.

He hadn't read the texts. I told him to, and his mum was saying that she didn't mean what she said, she'd had a bad day, would he come home.

'So what are you going to do?' I asked him. It was getting darker now. The blue of the sky deepened and the street lights came on, little pools of yellow on the paved path.

'She hasn't said sorry,' Jimmy noted. Which was true.

Yet, at that moment, I really felt he was on the verge of going back home. I knew I couldn't tell him what to do either way. I took his hand and squeezed it and he returned the pressure. Why did I do that? Because I felt sorry for him, I guess. Yeah. His results, the row with his mum, and knowing about Sophie. Who would never have taken time out from her busy schedule of hair straightening and lipgloss application to sit by the canal bank and chat to her boyfriend.

Jimmy got another text then. It was from his dad, asking if he'd had his results yet.

'The end of a beautiful relationship,' Jimmy muttered, as he texted the bad news back to his dad.

In a few minutes the reply came back. *Never mind. We'll sort it. Fancy coming over for dinner?*

'I'm going,' Jimmy said – no hesitation.

'Are you sure?' I asked him. 'It might be better to sort things out with your mum first.'

'I'll do that tomorrow.'

I could understand how Jimmy was feeling. One parent had given him a right bollocking, while the other was acting like some fairy godfather or something. A totally bizarre situation – one that would mess up anyone's head. I watched Jimmy text back his dad to say to expect him.

Then I said to him, 'Has Sophie been in touch?'

He shook his head but said they were going to see each other tomorrow. This is where I began to act stupidly.

'Did you miss her while she was away?'

'Yeah, course.'

'Did she get in touch from Majorca?'

'No – her phone didn't work over there.'

Which is absolute rubbish. Me and Maggie went to Majorca two years ago and when I got there, my phone reset itself to some phone company called Movistar and I was able to text all my friends.

I said, 'We're mates, aren't we?'

'Yeah,' he said. 'Who'd have thought it? Me and you.'

'Because you know you can talk to me about anything – even Sophie.'

The atmosphere went all funny then. He didn't really twig what I was on about, and I realised I'd inadvertently given him the impression that he could talk about his love life with other girls to me, when really what I wanted was . . .

I'm not going to go there right now. I'll just finish off what happened by the canal. Jimmy turned, looked at me and gave me a smile that changed his face completely. Usually his eyes dart around – he gives the impression of being uncertain, defensive but eager to please at the same time. Fooling around is his answer to everything. But now he was different. He smiled at me as if he knew something about me. And get this – my knees went weak. My stomach tightened. And I felt shy – like I wasn't sure what to say next and both wanted to be a million miles away from him but at the same time, wanted to stick like glue.

'You're really bothered about Sophie, aren't you?' he said, laughter in his voice.

I shrugged. I didn't know what to say to extricate myself from this.

Jimmy just threw me a huge grin, then put an arm around me, and gave me a squeeze. He said he'd better get along to his dad. I responded by saying my mates would wonder where I was. That's when he asked me about my results, so I told him what I'd got.

'Fantastic!' he said, looking delighted, not a trace of jealousy. 'You must be so made up!'

'A bit,' I said.

We walked back into town and I said goodbye to him outside the floodlit lobby of a bank's headquarters. There was a night porter there, sitting by the desk doing a crossword.

Jimmy said, 'Thanks, Liz. You're the best. I mean it.'

'Piss off,' I said to him.

Unbelievably, the next thing I did was text my friends to say I wasn't meeting them – my mum wanted to take me out. Instead I walked to the bus stop and took the bus home.

So here I am in my room recording all of this. And I have to ask myself, how *do* I feel about Jimmy now?

Answer – I feel sorry for him. The situation with his parents stinks, and he was disappointed with his results. And to know that Sophie has cheated on him – well, that's a time bomb ticking away for him. I am so going to be there to pick up the pieces.

But that's not all. The truth is that if while we were by the canal, Jimmy had made a move, I would have responded. I wanted to feel him close to me. Like, if he'd have kissed me, I'd have kissed him back. I'd have made him cheat on Sophie – and then I'd have been just as bad as her.

I'm beginning to see now how emotion is stronger than reason. It's no use me telling myself not to fancy Jimmy. I do fancy him, and there's an end of it. Even though he's not my type, even though we have nothing in common – when I'm with him I lose my sense of being in control – I feel like I'm a kid again. I get all awkward and clumsy. I'm ashamed of myself, only what I want to do now is think over every little thing that happened tonight, and remember it all – for ever.

Time to pull myself together. Whatever my feelings might be, I can do precisely nothing about them. Jimmy is going out with Sophie. And even then, he's got other problems. All I can do is stick around and keep an eye out for him.

With a bit of luck, he'll be on my shift tomorrow.

JIMMY

I wake up in the morning and for a split second I don't know where I am. The light in the room is soft and muted – there's no window. I'm tangled in a sheet that smells brand-new, as if someone has just taken it out of its packet. I'm in my dad's apartment. In the spare bedroom. When I open my eyes fully I see a white wall facing me, a white wall to my left, a white wall to my right, and on the floor, my sports bags, my old clothes scattered around, and my washbag lying open. I listen hard and think I can hear the sound of a radio playing in the distance. I'd like to turn over and go back to sleep, but I can't. I reach down and check my phone. Nine forty-five a.m.

I flashback to last night when I arrived here and my dad had made a fry-up for me – sausages, chips, beans, eggs – the lot. He presented it to me on a tray with a bottle of lager and he instructed me just to eat. And I did. Every last scrap. I asked him if he was mad about my results and he shook his head vigorously. He said he was no angel when he was my age. It wasn't his job to judge, but to help me find a way through. And that we'd talk in the morning.

When I'd finished eating, I noticed a shiny, black hardback book under the glass of the coffee table: *The Story of Film*. I asked him where he'd got that from. He said he'd bought it – he thought he'd better gen up on my main interest, and that I was welcome to have it when he'd finished. He said, did I know that the English pioneered moviemaking – apparently there was some chap from Leeds who made cameras and another bloke who was responsible for the first action and narrative shots? Then we just spoke about cinema, until we turned in. And he'd made up my bed and said if I liked we'd go out in the morning and get some new clothes. He said, have you left your mother? I said, I suppose – for a while. He nodded. He asked if I'd been in contact and I told him I'd texted to say I was OK.

End of flashback. I am doubly disorientated – that I should have left home so quickly, almost without meaning to, and that I have these two parents like Mr Good and Mrs Evil. I see my mum as the witch in *Snow White* and smile. She was one scary woman. And my dad as the fairy god-mother in *Cinderella*, which makes me smile even more. I swing out of bed and head for the bathroom.

In the shower I think of Liz. I smile even wider. There's no doubt about it – she's jealous of Sophie. I reckon she has been right from the start. The idea of Liz fancying me is the craziest thing I could possibly think of. I laugh, and luckily the sound is drowned by the rush of water. As I lather up I think of Liz and do you know – she is quite sexy. Not in the obvious way that Sophie is. But you could imagine that if a girl like that was actually into you – boy! Since I am naked in the shower I have to quickly start thinking of something else. I tell myself my dad is in the next room, that I'm on late shift at Coffee Corp, and even though things are good with me and my dad, there's still the mess of my results and my mum. I calm down.

Luckily the shower's protected by a solid screen rather than a curtain, but then showers always remind me of Janet Leigh in *Psycho*. So I pretend to scream and slowly sink to my knees in the shower like she does, covered in blood. I realise I'm in a good mood.

Dad's made breakfast. Bacon, eggs, tomatoes, fried bread. I tell him I'll start getting porky but he says I need to put on a bit of weight. He asks if I work out and I say I can't afford a gym subscription. I could have kicked myself. He smiles at me and says, he'll see what he can do.

After breakfast, we have the results conversation. I say, 'I know I could have put in more effort. But when—'

'What I'm interested in,' Dad said, cutting me off, 'is why no one noticed you weren't working. I don't mean Carol. I mean your teachers at your college.'

To be honest, quite a few of them had words and gave warnings, but it didn't seem to make any difference. It was more like there was something in me blocking them out. But I don't say that.

'Yeah, well, we're all supposed to be in charge of our own learning and that.'

Dad looks contemptuous. 'That's modern education for you. The teachers sit on their backsides and watch the students sink. What's your college called?'

'Westfield Sixth Form and Community College.'

'What's all that community business?'

I shrug. It's just a name, innit?

132

'Community? Typical of the jargon they use these days. I expect the staff are off on courses on Equality and Inclusion and suchlike.'

I don't know what he means, but I think I've seen those kind of words on notices around the place. And, yeah, it's jargon.

'They should be teaching the likes of you instead. But that's too much like hard work.'

I'm not going to stop Dad blaming college. I throw in what Liz said, about me making a fresh start elsewhere. Dad says it's an idea worth considering, and he'll make some enquiries. He tells me if I was brought on by the right sort of teachers, I'd do well. He knows it.

Sunlight pours in through the window fronting the street. I can't believe how lucky I am. Here's my dad like Superman stepping in and sorting it all out. It's funny, but up to now I didn't know I was missing having a dad. When Steve came along, it didn't bother me that we weren't related, and when the kids were born, I wasn't jealous. It was more like they just didn't have anything to do with me. But now I can see that my whole life would have been different if Mike had been along from the start. I think then that I know very little about the time he spent with my mum. Obviously they were incompatible. She said he was a bully. I can't see that myself.

I say, 'Did Mum throw you out, or did you leave?'

The question catches him on the hop. He puts down the mug of tea he's about to drink.

'Jimmy,' he says, 'I suppose I'm an old-fashioned kind of

bloke. I'm not going to pretend otherwise. I had traditional ideas about a marriage. That was part of the problem. But let me tell you something – I never, ever intended to leave you. You are my son. That flesh and blood tie means more to me than any other single thing. And this will surprise you. If I was to meet your mother again, if she was to accept me, if she wanted to make amends, and it happened that we got on, I wouldn't even rule out getting back with her. I loved her. She was my wife.'

I think, that would never happen in a million years. I feel sorry for my dad. I can see he's deluding himself a bit. But I'm touched by how much we mean to him. I feel secure, so I say, 'Were you ever violent towards her?'

'I would never, ever hurt a hair of that woman's head. There's a word for men who beat up women – thugs.'

'But she said—'

'Jimmy – let me tell you one thing about women. They can't always face the truth. Rather than admit they did something wrong, they'll tell themselves a version of the story in which they're blameless. They paint men as the villains – all the time. But women *are* the weaker sex. That's just the way it is.'

I think, I ought to introduce my dad to Liz and he'd soon change his mind. But he carries on talking.

'Speaking of which' – and he smiles knowingly – 'when am I going to meet this girlfriend of yours?'

'Sophie? Well, I'm seeing her tonight, I think.'

'Bring her round. I'll make myself scarce.'

I think, I might just do that. Dad carries on:

'Like I said last night, we'll go out and get you some decent clothes. Does Carol know you're living here?'

I'm living here? Well, I suppose I am. At least for a few days. I don't want to disappoint my dad, so I say, 'No sweat. I'll ring her this morning.'

'Good,' he says. Then he grins at me, and his grin's infectious. I grin back. It feels so good to have someone onside like this. My Dad. The best.

I'm speeding up the action now. We go to the Kingsgate Mall, me and my dad, into Gap, Nike, and he's helping me choose jeans, sweats, trainers and he says, you need a suit – every man should have a suit. I tell him I have one at home – I correct myself – at Carol's home, only the trousers are short in the leg. So – get this – he takes me into Paul Smith, and I try one, then another suit on – I don't recognise myself – then I check my watch and realise I have to be in work. Dad says, another day, and he takes the gear we've bought back to the – our – flat with him. My head's full of images of me in which I don't look anything like myself – standing in front of mirrors pulling cool faces, eyeing the clobber I'm modelling – it's like I can't quite catch up with what's happening.

Coffee Corp is a dose of normality. Liz is there. In the quiet times, and there aren't many of them, she asks me how I got on at my dad's, and I tell her. I keep watching her for signs she fancies me, but she's on the till and we're having to do without Amir today. So she's grinding coffee, heating paninis, shoving muffins onto plates and I have to keep my eye on the espresso machine. But once or twice I catch her looking at me and I wink back. When I do, she turns away and looks peeved. Girls. I'll never understand them.

I only get a ten-minute break but it's long enough to text my mum and tell her I'm staying with my dad for a while. I promise I'll call. Long enough also to text Sophie. She doesn't reply, but when I check my phone two hours later she says she'll meet me tonight. I text back straight away and say we'll go out for dinner – on me – and then back to my dad's flat. She texts back to say that's cool.

From that moment on my mind is firmly fixed on the night ahead. Me and Sophie in the apartment. We'll start off in the lounge, have a drink, and then after a few moves on the settee, I'll suggest the bedroom – or maybe it's too bare in there. Maybe better to close the blinds and make love on the rug. Nice one, Jimmy! The point about life, as well as films, is that it's the setting that counts. Setting creates mood. So I'll dim the lights, get something romantic on the music system – or maybe if there's a movie on TV we could leave it playing softly in the background.

'Jimmy! Where are the lattes I asked for?'

Damn. Double damn. Liz's voice smashes into my reverie. A dose of reality. Like the person in front of you in the cinema getting up and obscuring your view. I glance at her and she gives me an evil. I hastily revise my idea that she might fancy me.

Charlene comes out from the back now and joins Liz. As I plonk two lattes on the serving point I notice three spotty kids come in – well, lads of about thirteen, fourteen, I'd say. They're laughing, jostling each other. I keep an eye on them, watch them as they examine the stand with packets of coffee beans on sale.

But they come up to the till and speak to Liz.

'You got any Sprites?'

Charlene cuts in. 'No, just smoothies, or flavoured water.'

'Didn't ask you, you black bitch.'

That was a bit strong. Liz takes over.

'Out! Both of you. We don't have language like that in here.'

'Steady on,' Charlene says.

The boys throw a few insults at Liz, complain loudly that if we were a proper shop we'd have Sprites, and let off a few swear words as they exit. Customers tut, look away. Liz is spitting fire.

'I just hate kids like that! Haven't their parents taught them anything?'

'Hey, cool!' Charlene laughs. 'It happens – you get used to it.'

'How do you get used to it?' Liz says, off on one. 'How dare they think it's OK to talk like that? That's pure racism!'

I decide to tease her. 'Lighten up. They're just kids.'

'And kids grow up!' she countered, turning and facing me like it was me who made those remarks.

'Forget them. They're idiots,' I said.

'Which is exactly why you can't let them go unchallenged. If I'd had my way, I'd . . .'

'What? Flog them? Eat them alive? Grill them in a panini?'

'Shut up, Jimmy. This isn't something you can joke about.

Did you know, over in Belton—' She stopped herself. 'Well, whatever. I'd better go and help Charlene.'

She kills me, Liz. Takes everything way too seriously. They were just some brainless idiots. She goes on like they're the Ku Klux Klan. There's a queue at the till, and I'm kept at it solidly till the end of my shift.

When work is over, I leg it back to the flat, where I find Dad just finishing a call on his mobile. He ends the call and doesn't tell me who it was. I notice that because my mum always does. She puts down the phone and goes, that was Sandra – she needs a facial before next Tuesday – or – Jane's just told me her sister's got engaged. Or whatever.

I tell Dad about the arrangements with Sophie and he says he'll go out for a while if I want some privacy. Can you believe that? I grin at him and check he's got somewhere to go. He says he has some connections he needs to catch up with. Connections. Interesting. Then he looks a bit sheepish. He mutters, 'Jimmy, at your age I suppose I don't need to give you the usual father/son chat. You have got . . .'

It takes me a moment or two to get what he's on about. When I twig I feel myself going scarlet. 'Sure,' I say, fetching the packet from my jeans pocket. He smiles, rubs the back of his neck in embarrassment.

I meet Sophie at the station and she's looking awesome – in a tiny skirt showing her tanned legs and a pink top that stops short of four inches of scrummy midriff. When I hug her and tell her how gorgeous she looks she goes, not here! I back off. She can be moody at times, Sophie.

I bide my time. I take her to this Italian Dad recommended

and I tell her she can have anything she wants. She chooses garlic bread for starters and salmon – the most expensive dish on the menu. I order a bottle of wine and both of us are drinking it rather quickly. I can't keep my eyes off her – the way she holds the wine glass in mid-air, the way a black bra strap peeps out shyly from her top – my eyes zoom in on that – and her long, manicured nails, glistening with pink polish.

We don't talk much. We pass over results pretty quickly and she goes on a bit about Majorca while I half listen. I shovel the food – which is not half bad – into my mouth while I'm planning the rest of the evening. There's a mirror on the wall near us and every so often Sophie glances at it and checks her reflection. I find I'm copying her, and soon we're both of us looking into the mirror, watching ourselves eat and talk. This really is like the movies.

I'm getting horny now – and nervous. I pay the bill, leave a huge tip, and only then does the waiter start grovelling and showing us out. Soon I'm back at the apartment, and Sophie stops in the atrium to look around her.

'It's so cool here!' she exclaims. 'I love all those galleries above, and those cute little walkways. It's like Italy or somewhere like that.'

Italy? I'm encouraged as she isn't making any sense, which means the wine is affecting her. I steal a quick kiss and taste the garlic on her breath. I let her into the flat. As we walk into the lounge Dad gets up off the settee and gives Sophie the old once-over. I can tell immediately he likes what he sees. They shake hands and he asks her the usual polite questions – where she lives – what her ambitions are – then, as he promised, he says he has to go out. And ten minutes later, we're alone.

The moment has come. I walk over to the light switch and dim the light. Sophie is looking at the CDs so I go and join her. My dad's collection is pretty naff – there's lots of classical music – Elgar, Handel, a Classic FM collection of British Classics – and some early Stones and Beatles. I suggest we put on MTV. Sophie agrees.

She won't settle. She's walking round the flat, looking at everything. She says she loves it all, she adores the white leather settee, the conservatory area is amazing, the kitchen is so cute it's not true – she even steps up into it and opens drawers and peers inside.

'So you're staying here with your dad?' she asks.

'For the foreseeable future,' I tell her, and put an arm round her waist. She wriggles away and goes back into the lounge.

'Your dad doesn't mind me being here?'

'He trusts me,' I say. 'Big mistake!' I lunge at her and start nibbling at her neck. She squeals and says it makes her skin go funny. I stop her talking with a long, probing kiss.

It's beginning. While I'm concentrating on how fast to go here, I'm thinking of movie scenes where the hero and heroine get it together – that sequence in *Captain Corelli*, when she lets him have it in the fields, dying for it, not able to help herself. Or – yeah – *Fatal Attraction* – Michael Douglas and Glenn Close in the lift, and in the kitchen, and just about everywhere.

I notice I'm breathing heavily. I pull Sophie down onto

the floor and start stroking her thigh. I murmur to her how beautiful, how gorgeous she is. I can't believe it – here we are alone, and I really think it's going to happen. I realise I don't know whether Sophie is a virgin or not but I don't want to ask her. I prefer to let my hands do the talking.

She whispers to me, 'I *love* this apartment!'

I insert my hand under her top and cup her breast over her bra. She doesn't resist. Time to get under the bra. I'm doing well but notice vaguely Sophie is just letting me do this stuff, she's not really into it. Her eyes are open. I kiss her some more.

She says, 'The downlighting on the ceiling is lovely. My mum wanted to get the same sort for the kitchen but it was too expensive.'

I have hold of her left breast. I move my left hand up her thigh and just as I reach the edge of her knickers, her phone announces the arrival of a text. She pushes me away.

'Can't that wait?' I ask her.

Apparently not. While she reads it, I secretly undo my jeans. She smiles to herself at the text, a secret smile. I'm just a bit put out.

'Who's that from?' I ask her.

'Oh? That? Oh – it's just Liz!'

'Liz? What did she want?'

'Oh, nothing. Girlie stuff.'

Sophie gets up now, saying she's thirsty and she's going to look in the kitchen for something to drink.

That bloody Liz! Just when I was getting somewhere. One day I'll get her back for this. But for now my eyes are fixed on

Sophie in the kitchen, pulling down her skirt, opening the fridge and getting out the Diet Coke. I join her in the kitchen. I wait while she pours herself a drink.

When she's finished I grab her immediately and push her against the corner where the fridge meets the cupboard. I thrust myself up against her. I kiss her over and over again. I'm getting desperate now.

'Do you wanna come to the bedroom?' I mutter.

'OK,' she says.

Yesssssss!

I lead her by the hand out into the corridor and she opens the door to my dad's room.

I warn her. 'That's my dad's room.' The door to my room is at right angles to his. I show her.

'It's much smaller than your dad's room,' she tells me. 'Hold on – I need the bathroom.'

She vanishes. I can hardly contain myself. Maybe there are things girls need to do before sex. I wait and wait. And wait. She emerges looking immaculate, her phone in her hand.

'I had to make some calls,' she said. 'And I hope you don't mind, I've rung for a taxi. I have to be in work early tomorrow. But I've had a lovely time, Jimmy.'

Disappointment sluices through me. Everything sags.

'You've only just got here,' I tell her.

'I've spent the whole evening with you,' she said, and now approaches me and starts kissing me. In between kisses she talks to me. 'I do like you, Jimmy. You're cute.' More kisses. She pats my trousers, notices they're undone, and does them up for me. 'It's just that I want to take things slowly, if that's all right with you. But you are sooo tasty!' She kisses me long and deep. 'It's hard for me too, you know.'

She breaks away. 'Your dad seems nice. Cool of him to let us have the flat. Do you think he will again?'

'Yeah!' I say.

'Well, maybe I'll stay longer next time.'

The entryphone rings. Her cab has arrived. I walk her down to the entry, kiss her goodbye, and watch the cab depart.

I reckon I'm making progress here. At least I think I am. Maybe. Whatever.

LIZ'S DIARY

Saturday 18th August

Eighth entry

I think I'll have to say something.

This is why. I was standing at the bus stop this morning on my way into Coffee Corp when Sophie arrived by my side. As luck – bad luck? – would have it, she was going in to work at the same time as me. I couldn't think of an excuse to use to get away from her, so we ended up hip to hip on the double seat at the front of the bus. And then she began.

'Have you seen Jimmy's dad's apartment? I went there last night. It's so cool! It's just like one those makeover dream homes on telly! The kitchen fittings were gorgeous – the drawers shut automatically and the tap in the sink unit is one of those where you just lift a lever . . .' And she was away. How can anyone be so interested in décor? I blanked out most of what she said.

'To be honest, Liz, I was thinking of dumping him, but after last night, I'm having second thoughts. And – omigod! – while we were snogging I get a text from Mark – a really romantic one – shall I show you?'

'No, no,' I say hastily.

'But it was all right – Jimmy didn't find out – don't look so upset – actually, I told him the text was from you – but you won't split on me, will you? We girls must stick together!'

I was speechless. But I did manage to ask her:

'Then who exactly *are* you going out with?'

'Oh, Liz! Well, Jimmy, I suppose, as Mark lives so far away – except he's said I should go and spend a weekend with him – and I will. Jimmy *is* kind of cute and he's so desperate to go to bed with me, which is sweet of him. And like I said, I love his dad's flat. And he's living there permanently now. I can go round whenever I want. And I met his dad – he's adorable!'

'Adorable?'

'Yeah! Kind of . . . You know . . . like a dad.'

I reckon the reason Sophie can't express herself is not that she's thick – far from it, she's a cunning little schemer – but she's so focussed on herself, she doesn't notice anything about anyone else. Now if I'd met Jimmy's dad . . .

'So, anyway, I reckon I'll keep Jimmy hanging on for a while until I see how things with Mark develop. It's better having a boyfriend than not having one, isn't it? Oh – sorry, Liz. I forgot about you! You don't have anyone. I'm so stupid sometimes. But you could have any bloke you wanted – if you tried.'

'What *are* you saying? That I don't try hard enough?'

'No! The opposite – I so admire you! Because you're so independent – you don't need a man in your life.'

I thought, I certainly don't need *you* in my life, but I

145

didn't say it. Instead I just sat there fuming. Luckily an old lady got on the bus then, and there were no seats, so I jumped up from mine and insisted she sat down. I noticed Sophie wriggle away from her.

We were run off our feet at work, and I was glad. I was still processing all that Sophie had told me, and was reaching the conclusion that the only option I had was to tell Jimmy. Only I wasn't prepared to yet. Each time he smiled at me, I kind of deflected his smile. I froze him out. I didn't want to, but I was so conscious of the mess Sophie had made – not just of their relationship, but of me and Jimmy's relationship. When I told him the truth, he would hate me. What is it they say? Don't shoot the messenger? I'm going to have to be the messenger. As the day went on, my mood became fouler and fouler. Even Bob commented that I had to watch out otherwise I'd curdle the milk. Cheers, Bob.

I knew I needed to speak to someone about the whole Sophie/Jimmy/me situation, and who better than Maggie and Peter? That night Peter arrived with a Chinese takeaway and we all three sat on the sofa and tucked in. Afterwards I said to both of them:

'If you had a friend and you knew their partner was cheating on them, would you tell?'

They thought about it. Maggie said, 'That's tough. It's a question of where your loyalties lie. Your friend wouldn't thank you if they ever found out you *knew* they'd been made to look a fool.'

'Yeah,' I said, rubbing at a sweet and sour sauce stain on my jeans. 'That's what I think.'

'On the other hand,' said Peter, 'you should never interfere in other people's relationships.'

'Don't give me that!' Maggie turned on him. 'Look at you talking – the investigative journalist! You spend your professional life interfering in other people's business and whistle-blowing!'

Peter laughed. But I was glad she'd said that. I'd never really spoken properly to Peter about his job, and journalism was something I'd often considered for myself. Also I wondered if we could draw him out on his Belton assignment. I thought I'd better take it step by step.

'What does that mean exactly – an investigative journalist? What is it you do?'

'Your mum's exaggerating a bit – I'm basically just a news reporter. But a lot of my job is about ringing around chasing stories, finding out if certain rumours are true.'

'Come on!' Maggie interrupted. 'Tell her about the double glazing company you exposed.'

'OK. It was last year. You might have read about it. Apex Glass. Their salesmen targeted the elderly, giving them the hard sell, and also implying that Apex had a connection with the local authority, and if they ordered windows they could get a grant to cover the full amount, provided they laid down a hundred pounds cash deposit. Which naturally they never saw again. And there was more. But I shan't bore you with it.'

Maggie carried on. 'So Peter got his mum to pretend to order something from Apex, bugged the conversations, and wrote a big exposé in his paper. Even radio and TV picked it up.'

'Cool!' I said. 'You must have been pleased with yourself.'

'Yes,' Peter said reflectively. 'That was good. But sometimes you end up hounding people when you'd rather not. It's a mixed job. But good if you're fundamentally nosy, like I am.'

'There's another investigation underway, isn't there,' Maggie added. 'Tell Liz about that.'

'He has done.' I gave Maggie a superior smile. She looked baffled. Me and Peter shared a secret that she wasn't in on. But not for long. I explained how he'd dropped into Coffee Corp and what he'd told me. Maggie looked very, very pleased.

'You can see how important it is now,' she babbled. 'Not just because of Peter's job – but the by-election. And in general terms – anything you can do to combat racism is good. They have this façade, all these reasonable white blokes, only concerned about Great Britain, but really it's all about kicking out immigrants – I mean black and Asian immigrants. And there's nothing they wouldn't stoop to.'

We all agreed, all three of us. And just then we were a unity. I liked the feeling.

Confession time. Despite everything I wrote at the beginning of this diary, I have to admit that Peter's all right. I am getting used to him. Also, it's good to see Maggie looking so happy. No – more than happy – she's lit up inside. Even when she's not with Peter, she's different, somehow. She doesn't lose her temper, she sees the funny side of things – she smiles – smiles more than I can ever remember.

I'm not jealous any more of Peter. How could I be? But I'm remembering what Sophie said to me, about me being independent. And yeah – it is good to be able to rely on yourself. But it's also lonely. And Maggie hasn't been diminished by the fact Peter is in her life. She's even more herself, her best self. I want that for me too.

Except I won't have it. I've realised that if I do get Jimmy to question his feelings for Sophie, it means I can never go out with him. Otherwise I'm as low-down and scheming as she is. The fact is, if I'm his friend – then I have the right to tell him Sophie is bad news. But if I'm a potential girlfriend, then to tell him about Sophie would be an act of manipulation. All that is really clear to me.

Jimmy and I aren't ever going to get together. There'll be no going to see a movie with him, and hearing him go on endlessly about it. No sitting with him on a bench down by the canal again, isolated in our own universe. No having to put up with Bob, Amir and Charlene's amusement when they find out we're an item. No bringing him back home for Maggie to meet, no having him over here for a takeaway and seeing what he thinks of Peter, and Peter of him. I may as well imagine it all, because I know it ain't never going to happen. Jimmy is like my private fantasy, a film in my head. In the real world, we'll have to stay apart.

Sunday 19th August

Ninth entry

World War Three has broken out.

It happened at five p.m. this afternoon, once we'd closed

down for the day. Charlene hurried off to meet her twin sisters who'd been drumming with the steel band in Exchange Square. That left me and Jimmy. I knew I had to seize the moment.

'Fancy a coffee?' I asked him.

'A coffee is the last thing I fancy right now,' he joked.

'OK. Well, what about a drink? We can go across the road to Jaguar.'

The bar looked inviting. It wasn't too busy, and a sudden breeze had whipped up around us, possibly heralding rain.

Jimmy said, 'You just can't wait to get me on your own, can you?'

I knew he was flirting with me and I forced myself not to respond.

'Come on,' I said. 'The green man's flashing.' I pulled him over the road.

We got a table by the window. We'd both ordered cold beer and drank it from the bottle. There was a low thump of background music. I still wasn't sure how to begin what I had to say. So I played for time.

'How are things with your dad?' I asked him.

Jimmy's eyes met mine. He has intelligent, expressive eyes, which can change from thoughtful to mischievous in an instant. Now he was just happy to share with me.

'Dad's great – it's Mum that's causing the hassle. She's insisting I go and see her back home tomorrow.'

'Are you going?'

'Yeah.' He was resigned. 'I need to fetch some more things over to the flat, anyway.'

'So you're going to live with your dad permanently?'

'For a bit.'

'But what will you do if your mum apologises and begs you to go back to her?'

Jimmy screwed up his face and took another slug of beer. 'That's not very likely, is it?'

'But what if she only said those things in the heat of the moment and regrets them?'

Jimmy thought for a moment. 'Yeah, well, in that case we can all be friends. That's OK. But I still feel I'd like some time to get to know my dad. Know what I mean?'

'Are you sure it's not his money talking at you?'

'What is this, an interrogation?'

I could see I'd riled him, and that certainly wasn't my intention. I can be so ham-fisted sometimes.

'Sorry, Jimmy. I just ... well, anyone would be seduced by all that cash. I know I would be! Most definitely. But I can see you're also catching up on lost time. What else have you found out about your dad? Tell me.'

I could see he looked a bit happier.

'Not a lot. He's more interested in me all the time. We talk about me. He's told me a little bit about his childhood – and he says he's a bit old-fashioned.'

'That's good,' I told him, wanting to make him feel better. 'Sometimes parents try to be cooler than us and it's so embarrassing. Give me an old-fashioned parent any time. One who you can shock!'

We both laughed. Harmony was restored. God, I thought, I so like being with him! I just feel so comfortable. For a moment – for quite a few moments – I almost decided not to drop the Sophie bomb on him. I didn't want to spoil this. We could have another drink, and maybe a third. And then . . . And then . . .

'I thought I'd shock him when I brought Sophie round on Friday night,' Jimmy went on. 'But he seemed to like her. Shook her hand and that. He even left us alone together.'

I came down to earth with a bump. The time had come.

'How was your night with Sophie?' Someone had turned off the music in the bar. It seemed deathly quiet.

Jimmy looked a bit embarrassed. Then he suddenly grinned at me. 'You've got a cheek!' he said. 'Texting Sophie while we were getting it on.'

'I didn't text her,' I said.

'You did – how can you deny it?'

'Because I didn't text her. She just said I did.' I kept my voice even, neutral. I watched Jimmy put his hand round his bottle ready to lift it to his mouth. But he didn't – he let go of it, flashed me a quizzical look, and looked a bit lost.

'She said it was you.'

The music started up again. My stomach was in knots. I hated myself.

'So who was it?' Jimmy frowned. I lost my nerve.

'It doesn't matter. Have you seen the latest Jim Carrey movie? The one where he's playing a straight guy? The reviews make it sound interesting.'

'I don't get this. How do you know about all of this stuff about that text?'

'Because I saw Sophie on the bus yesterday morning. But it doesn't matter.'

'It does matter.' Now he gripped my hand. I was quaking. I bitterly regretted getting involved in this. For the first time I was seeing that always telling the truth wasn't such a good idea.

'Ignore me,' I said. 'You know I'm not Sophie's biggest fan.'

Jimmy let go my hand and visibly relaxed. 'You're jealous!' he exclaimed, delighted.

'Yeah, whatever.'

'Liz!' He grinned at me, a wide grin. 'Shit!' He laughed a while. 'Hey, listen, this thing with Sophie. I know we're going out and that, but it's not serious, know what I mean?'

'You're not in love with her?'

'No way. Shall I get us some more beer?'

'In a moment. I'm glad you're not involved with her, because she's not got a good track record – she's a bit of a player.'

He smiled at me again. But less certainly. I could see his mind working. Like I've said, Jimmy's a bit of a dreamer, but he's all there. I could tell from the expression on his face something had clicked.

'Do you mean that text was from another bloke?'

I shrugged.

'Tell me,' he said.

'Someone she met on holiday.'

He went very still. Very quiet. I didn't like seeing Jimmy like that.

'I wouldn't have told you, except I know she's dragged me into this, and I didn't want to be part of a lie. But I'm sure there's nothing in it. It was only a text.'

He still didn't say anything. I just wanted to hug him tight and make him feel better. But I couldn't. We each sat there, miles apart, locked in our respective misery.

After a while, he said, 'My dad's right.'

'Right about what?' I jumped in.

'Right about women. Being liars. Being the weaker sex.'

'Jimmy!' I was outraged. 'He said *that*?! Does he live in the Dark Ages or something?'

'Lay off my dad!' he shouted at me. He shouted at me!

'Watch it!' I shouted back, even louder. Everyone in the bar, as well as the bar staff, looked over at us. I didn't care. I stood up, knocking over my chair, and pointed at Jimmy.

'Don't have a go at me just because you're angry with Sophie! I'm being your friend, OK? I'm being honest with you. And what your dad says stinks. And you know it. Just watch out that you don't get involved in some sort of old hate-match between your mum and your dad. And if you do, and if you get into trouble,' I said through gritted teeth, 'remember I'm here for you!! And for the record, I *don't* fancy you. But you can count on me, OK?'

'Drop your voice,' he said. The guy behind the bar beckoned to one of the bouncers. They were closing in on us. I threw an evil look at the bouncer. A big mistake. He came over and spoke to Jimmy.

'Is this young lady bothering you?'

'Yeah,' he said. 'But I can—'

'Out!' he said to me.

'You bastard!' I shouted – and I didn't know whether I meant the bouncer or Jimmy or both. I grabbed my bag, and my head held high, I marched out of the bar.

Marched out of the bar, got the bus home, and went straight to my room. And wrote this.

Jimmy will never speak to me again. Nor will Sophie. Nor will I ever go back to the Jaguar, which is – was – one of my favourite bars. I could scream with humiliation and the unfairness of it all. Because I was only trying to do the right thing.

I don't know who I hate most – Jimmy, Sophie or me.

Probably me.

JIMMY

Late August is the worst time of year. The summer is fed up with being summer, and even the leaves on the trees are hanging around bored. September – and the beginning of term – is just around the corner and do you know? You're almost glad it's coming because August has become so stale.

So if I was shooting a really depressing movie, that's when I'd set it. Late August. The road where I used to live is lined with old trees whose roots have blistered the paving stones. Years ago, when I was a kid, I used to get excited when some of them let drop glistening chocolate-brown conkers. All that's gone.

All's loss. My future – what future? – my girlfriend – my mate Liz – all gone. I kick an empty can and listen to it clatter along the street. I slow down, reluctant to walk up my old front path. I like the image – the dented can limping more and more slowly to a halt in the gutter. Like me. Right now my dad doesn't seem real – I can feel myself being sucked back into my mum's world, this old house, sending out invisible rays, surrounding and squeezing me, drawing me in.

I decide that being in a crap mood is actually rather good for my creativity.

I'm going to be firm. I have the speech all planned out in my mind. How I don't want there to be any animosity between us but for my sake I have to move on. I'm staying with my dad for a bit. No hard feelings. Maybe it's better like this. We'll always have Paris. That's from *Casablanca* – great movie. Just now I have the camera shooting me from behind, maybe at waist height, so you can watch my footsteps moving inexorably closer to my old front door.

Which magically opens and there is Kyle.

'Jimmy! Jimmy!' He flings himself at me and wraps his legs round my waist. I've forgotten how good it is to feel a kid clinging to you, squirming and wriggling and chattering away.

'They got me a swing in the garden and it goes so high and I can make it go nearly over my own head. And we was in the garden yesterday and we saw a frog-thing which was dead and they said the cat got it. And—'

Mum's coming to the door now. I disentangle myself from Kyle who skitters away back to the garden. Mum looks pale and thin. My throat feels dry and I try to swallow. I see the lines around her eyes and the pallor of her lips. For the first time I realise I might have hurt her. I don't like that feeling, don't like it at all. So I try to remind myself of all the stupid things she said to me last time we were together, but they seem worn out and irrelevant now. I don't understand how all this could have happened. I just want to be friends.

It's Steve who takes control. He says he's brewed some tea and we should come into the kitchen to talk. Silently we all do. Mum sits at the kitchen table and begins to fold up the newspaper. Steve busies himself with the tea. Mum asks me some polite questions – how am I? Do I have enough money? Was it any cooler outside?

I try smiling at her but my face muscles aren't working properly. Eventually Steve brings us over our drinks and sits down with us. This feels like some kind of family board meeting. Yes. An Extraordinary General Meeting of the Keane family. Normally when I make jokes to myself, I smile inside. But now I can't. Instead I feel awkward, confused and just plain bad. I think they call the feeling, guilt.

Steve opens: 'I'm glad you're here. I think we all need to clear the air.'

Then Mum cuts in. 'Jimmy – listen – I'm sorry for the things I said to you. I was harsh. I take them back.'

The speech I'd prepared disperses like a lifting mist. I say nothing.

'I was frustrated as I think I saw your bad grades coming. But even then, I should have trodden more carefully. But I think – I've been talking this through with Steve – that maybe I was angry at you for other reasons.'

I remember what Liz said and add, 'Like I'd been seeing my dad, and you felt you were losing control.'

She looks surprised and glances at Steve. He seems taken aback too. I privately resolve to thank Liz for that – then remember she will probably never talk to me again as long as she lives.

Mum says, 'I'm glad you understand. So forget I ever said those things. And also, I want to you to know this is your home, and you can come back here any time, and we shan't ask you any questions or even make a fuss. We'll just carry on as before.'

Steve nods vigorously. My guess is that the low key re-entry is his idea. It has Steve's fingerprints all over it.

'OK,' I said. 'Thanks. And I'm sorry for losing my rag too, and for storming out.'

Mum throws me a sad smile. She sips at her tea. Then she begins again. 'There's one other thing. I've been thinking long and hard about this. Jimmy – I'm not happy about you getting involved with your father. Not because I'm jealous, though I am, and not because I think you can't look after yourself. But I don't trust him.'

I feel myself prickle defensively.

'So I've decided to tell you everything. The choice of who you live with is yours, yours entirely. But it's only fair to give you all the facts.'

'My dad's been very good to me,' I tell her. I think about all the money he's lavished on me, all that new gear that I still feel strange in – and how Liz said it was money talking.

'I'm glad he's been good to you,' Mum says.

I don't want to hear what's coming. I don't want to find out anything bad about my dad. We're getting on really well. Last night after I'd got back from Jaguar I was all churned up. I risked it and told my dad what had happened. He said to chuck Sophie – that she was no good. He gave me the push I needed. He said that Liz had done me a favour and he remembered her from the first time he'd come into Coffee Corp. Said she wasn't the right sort of girl for me, but

OK as a friend. He took me to the movies and we sat in those exclusive seats where you can drink beers during the film. When we got home we microwaved some food and watched TV till late. Just before I turned off the light in my room he stood at the door to wish me goodnight. He stayed there for a moment, gazing at me. I don't want my mum to scribble furiously all over that picture. I don't want her making it all turn sour.

'I don't need to know about the past,' I tell her.

'We all need to know about the past,' she says. 'It's the only way to avoid making mistakes in the future.'

'Your mother's not being vindictive,' Steve adds. 'She just wants you to be fully informed.'

'But how do I know she won't distort everything?' I turn on Steve.

'She won't,' he says.

I'm trapped. I have no choice but to listen. And as she starts to speak I find myself thinking, this is also just a film – a kind of prequel to my dad's film, her version of events. Only this time my mum's the director and the producer, she's starring, and she'll be casting my dad as the villain.

I'm listening to her and I'm watching. Opening credits stand out against the black and white backdrop of the city before the modernisation programme – dirty streets, old-fashioned department stores, phone boxes on street corners as there were no mobiles . . .

First scene. There's Mum coming out of college and there's Dad, waiting for her, a wilting bunch of flowers in his hand. He's been there ages, happy because he knew she was inside. She comes out and his face lights up. Maybe the two of them are technicolour against the grey street, just for a moment. Just one moment.

The next sequence is my mum and Gran. They're shouting at each other. My mum, tearful, impassioned, explaining how much she was in love, how she was going to get married whatever anyone said. Gran's face stony, lips pursed. Mum pleads with her, explains that Mike has money, enough to set them up in a flat, enough to get them started in life. Gran's kitchen – where they're standing – is cramped – there's a square wooden table in the middle separating Mum and Gran. It's an image – they're set in opposition, they can't reach each other.

And then it's the wedding – it takes place in a local church. My mum swathed in white, Dad in a suit, white also with nerves. What's driving him is this absolute determination to have Mum. And her, helpless, like a victim. I can hear the wedding march being played. The vicar beams. Someone in the congregation coughs. Mum's voice-over goes, *the wedding was like a dream – almost like it was happening to someone else. I even remember thinking as I said my vows, was this really me?*

In films about broken marriages, you know right from the first frame it's not going to work out.

Their first big argument. That's what comes next. Just before he's about to switch on the telly, she asks him a question, far too casual. Could she could join her college mates on one of their nights out in town?

DAD: No.

MUM: What do you mean, no?

DAD: You're not going and that's final. You're my wife. I should be enough for you.

That scene was in Dad's film. She was the one who wanted out. They were incompatible. Which means no one was to blame. I'm learning nothing new. I watch the rest of the film unfold, unconcerned.

Now they're in their bedroom, getting ready for a night in the pub with their friends. He's telling her to tie back her hair and to go easy on the make-up. *We don't want you looking like some tart*, he says, not unkindly.

And here he is tearing a page from a notebook and telling her that's their meals for the week. He's asking her who she spoke to at college, checking on her. I notice how my mum's shooting only in their flat, their tiny, claustrophobic flat. For her the marriage was a prison. He was the jailer.

Now I see her coming out of college exhausted. Takes out that crumpled list from her pocket and the camera zooms in on 'shepherd's pie'. She grimaces. Later she gets off the bus by the flat and sees the local curry house, goes in, orders curry for two, waits in the flock-wallpapered waiting area by the side of the restaurant.

Gets home, lays out the curries on plates, waiting for Dad. He comes in, he's puzzled, sees the curries, scowls at her. Then his face scrunches up and he changes, he's overtaken by a rage that doesn't seem to belong to him. He accuses her of deliberately going against his wishes, she *knows* he can't stand stinking curries.

She shouts at him to behave himself – camera zooms in on each of their faces, ugly, screaming – and then she tells me he picks up a plate and hurls it at the wall. I watch brown, glutinous sauce and chunks of meat slide down over the patterned wallpaper, triangular segments of smashed white plate mixed in with the mess. I'm shocked.

But this is not *my* dad.

In the next scene, he goes back to being my dad again. Mum's sobbing in the bedroom. He's beating at the door, saying he's sorry, again and again. Hey, he's crying too. She won't let him in. He walks away. And then – he summons all his force and runs at the door, a live battering ram, it smashes, and there he is in front of her. I flinch. But he's not violent, he hugs her, like he never wants to let her go.

He's kissing her. I don't want to watch any more. I wrest my attention away from the images and listen to my mum's words instead.

That was the night you were conceived, Jimmy.

So they had sex? Did he rape her? I'm confused, and a bit sick.

I was sick in the first few weeks, Mum says, and I'm forced back to this movie, the one I don't want to watch. She tells me that never, for one moment, did she not want me. *You were something separate from him, Jimmy. You were growing inside me.*

Now Dad's being kind to her again. In fact he can't do

163

enough for her. Look – he's bringing her a footstool so she can put up her feet. He's fetching her a cup of tea – the handle tiny in his huge fist. He puts his hand on her stomach and she laughs, says it's too early for him to feel anything yet. He's treating her like a princess. She looks happy again. It's as if they were waiting for me to come along to make it all right.

I'm born. There I am, a red, wrinkled thing wrapped in a blanket, and my mum's in bed, holding me in her arms, gazing at me. I'm staring at her. Our eyes are locked on each other. There's no dad in the picture. Mum takes her index finger and strokes the soft skin on my face. I turn my head, my mouth searching for her finger.

Now she directs the story of *my* life. I'm a naughty, noisy toddler. I'm crawling round, emptying cupboards, getting out saucepans, banging on them with wooden spoons. (Didn't they buy me any *real* toys? What is this?) Dad's playing with me, encouraging me, mock-wrestling with me. Mum looks happy, but exhausted.

Next scene. She's just put me down for an afternoon nap when the phone rings. A friend of hers offers her some part-time work. Mum's face lights up. That evening she tells Dad:

MUM: Just sixteen hours a week. Enough to give me a break and earn something decent. You know we're struggling with money.

DAD: If one of us has to work, Carol, that person will be me. I'll do extra hours.

MUM: But listen! Mum can look after Jimmy. He'll be fine.

DAD: He needs *you*. The trouble with you, Carol, is that you lack the maternal instinct. That's why you want to go to work. But you're not going, and that's final.

I'm siding with my mum, but then, that's her intention. I know all about how directors create bias, give sympathy to the devil.

Next it's a comic scene. They're watching the news on telly. Some item about having closer ties with Europe. Mum says she'd like that, she's always been attracted by the French and Italian lifestyles. He laughs at her, tells her she should be proud of being British. She laughs back.

'Admit you're wrong,' he tells her. 'Admit you're wrong.'

She gets up to leave the room, laughing. 'I'm not wrong,' she says. He gets up, lunges at her, pins her to the wall, she has to turn her head to one side. He's still laughing. But there's a dangerous glint in his eye. 'Admit you're wrong!'

She shouts at him to stop it. 'Admit you're wrong,' he says through gritted teeth. He presses himself against her. She's beating at him with her fists. He's immovable. She's scared now.

'OK,' she says, her breath coming in pants. 'I'm wrong.'

Maybe Dad was a bully. But he's changed, right?

When we get to the scene when she tells him she's leaving, I'm prepared for it. Mum announces that they would have to separate. I'm not in this scene. I'm forgotten already.

165

Dad rants and raves. He accuses her of having a lover. She screams, *where would I have the energy for one?* Then he changes tack and tells her she can go, go back to her mother, but I am staying with him. Mum refuses absolutely. They carry on arguing. In the end, both are so worn down they go to bed. I'm spark out in my kid's bed in another room. I'm just two years old.

In bed, they call a truce. Dad begs Mum to reconsider, tells her how much he loves her. She listens, accepts what he's saying, but he's the one that falls asleep and she lies there awake, eyes wide open, staring at the ceiling. Gets up, goes to the kitchen, lights up a cigarette and sits there as the dawn light presses at the window. Finally she goes back to bed, gets in, lies down, closes her eyes. Is she asleep? Impossible to tell.

Dad gets up and goes to work. Mum is asleep now – deeply asleep – she doesn't wake for another hour. When she gets out of bed, she looks different. Happier, somehow. She goes to me – I'm playing on my bedroom floor with some jigsaw puzzle. She scoops me up and hugs me tight. She cleans and feeds me, and takes me into her bedroom while she packs a suitcase.

She rings for a cab. Fifteen minutes later, the taxi driver hoots outside. Mum gets me into my jacket, takes me to the front door, then puts down the suitcase as she tries to open it. She can't. It's jammed. Nothing she can do will shift it. The cab driver carries on hooting. Mum rings the cab company back and explains the problem. Eventually the driver comes up to our front door and finds out the door is bolted from the outside. A makeshift affair, looks like it's only just been done. It was my dad. He'd locked us in.

With some help, the driver manages to free us and get us out. He drives us to my gran. Next scene, Dad's outside my gran's house pleading for us to come back to him, until they threaten to bring the police. The whole street can hear him. He calls my mum a traitor, a child-stealer, a whore.

No, he couldn't have. Not my dad.

It's nearly the end. Mum said he started harassing her on Gran's phone. Whatever they said, they couldn't make him hang up. He begged to speak to me but they wouldn't let him. Then one day the pestering just stopped. Later they found out he'd left the city. Mum didn't want to know where. She contacted a solicitor and arranged to get a divorce as soon as she could.

That's a pretty rubbish ending.

I listen to Mum as she finishes.

'Jimmy – maybe I was wrong, but I took the decision never to tell you any of this. I think it was partly selfish of me – I didn't want to have to relive the biggest mistake of my life. Also I didn't want you to think of yourself as the product of a mistake. I couldn't see what good it would do you, knowing that your father was so vile. We all believe the stories we're told about ourselves. I wanted to tell you a different story from the true one. I gave you a history that was only about me loving you, and us sticking it out together – until Steve came along. And Steve couldn't have been any more different from Mike.'

She throws him a grateful and a loving glance.

'I'm sorry, Jimmy. But now you know everything. I haven't left anything out.'

I can't process all this. It's lying like an undigested meal in my stomach, making me feel heavy and sick. I can't link up in my mind the Mike I know, eager to please, thoughtful, rather lonely, with the monster my mum has been describing. I know she's telling me the truth, but I know *I* know the truth too. If this was a movie . . . If it was *my* movie . . .

I can't think how my movie would go on from here.

I don't know what to do next.

I try a lame excuse. 'He's changed,' I said. 'You're talking about events from fifteen years ago.'

Steve takes that up. 'That's right. We don't know what experiences he's had in the past fifteen years. He must have moved on. But I suppose we're saying, just be careful.'

'Yes,' Mum says. 'Be careful.' Then she adds, 'Are you coming home?'

I want to say that I am. I can hear Kyle and Stacey laughing in the garden and I'd like to be out there with them, lifting Kyle in the air and turning him upside down. Then I think of my dad's apartment, how fresh and new it is, how he's fresh and new and how he could have changed – everyone changes – hell – *I'm* going to change. I've dumped Sophie and I'm going to work hard next year. Dad even said he'd get me a tutor.

The sudden ring of the doorbell cuts across my thoughts. Isn't this always the case? You're in the middle of a big family drama and the milkman calls to get paid. Or the kid next door has lobbed his ball into your back yard. It's like the end of *Brief Encounter*, when the lovers are making their last goodbye and that old lady comes and sits at their table, and starts up a conversation.

'I'll get it,' Steve says.

He disappears, and a few moments later, reappears. With my dad.

He's looking smart, neat and somehow smaller. Cowed and unsure of himself. That's because he won't look directly at anyone, and hangs his head just a little. Now I really can't connect the bully my mum told me about, and this quiet, middle-aged man. I watch my mum. She's gone white. I wonder then how much of her story was just exaggeration. We all exaggerate, don't we, when we want to get someone on our side? I look at my dad and discover it's impossible to think bad of someone when they're standing right in front of you.

My mum's a bit rude to him. She says, 'What's brought you here?'

He says, 'I don't want there to be any hard feelings between us, now that we all have to think about Jimmy.'

'There are no hard feelings,' she answers, without meeting his eye.

'And I wanted to say,' Mike adds, 'that you've done a wonderful job with him, Carol. He's a great kid. You've done us both proud.'

My mum looks astonished. I blush.

'And, Jimmy,' he goes on, 'where you live is your decision.'

Yesss! I think to myself. Dad is showing Mum and Steve

that he *has* changed. He's making it easy for me to go back to that cool life in his apartment. More and more I realise that Mum's story was only to do with the past – and even if it was all true, it's not going to repeat itself. Not now. Not ever.

I explain then that I'll probably stay with Dad a bit longer, at least until the beginning of term. I tell them it'll probably be easier for me to study without the distraction of the kids. I see Mum raise her eyebrows and I realise then another attraction of Dad – he really will let me turn over a new leaf. I tell Mum that Dad and I have been talking about me starting a new college – maybe the technology college in the city centre, where I can retake some modules and maybe do a course in film. I want to say more, but it's hard with Dad being there. I notice Mum has drawn closer to Steve. She's holding on to his arm.

I leave with Dad, but hug Mum first and shake Steve's hand. I tell them not to worry. Dad has a car outside – a Triumph sports model. He mentions he's renting it for a month. I am seriously impressed, slide into the passenger seat, and the cameras in my head start rolling again. Me and Dad setting off into the sunset. Both of us about to start a new life.

I don't tell him what my mum says. I find I just want to bury it deep. Instead we chat about trivial things. As we get further from my house his mood lightens. It's impossible to connect him sitting there, humming a tune, with my mum's Mike Leigh gritty realistic story of domestic abuse. The way he bullied her, stopped her from seeing her friends.

My mum's like me. She even admitted it. She has a tendency to make stuff up.

I say to Dad, 'Tell me if I'm out of order here, but could I invite some of my mates round? To the flat?'

He stops humming. I realise this is a test. Is he going to stop *me* having a social life? I hold my breath.

'A fantastic idea,' he says. 'Why don't you have a party?'

'Can I?'

'Sure.'

'And invite some girls?'

He laughs indulgently. 'That's my son.'

Immediately I'm planning it in my head. First I'll ask Liz – already I'm over what happened in Jaguar, and the fact that Sophie accepted her dismissal so happily proved to me she was no great loss. I reckon I'll have the whole crowd from Coffee Corp and their other halves. JC is the bloke Charlene lives with – he's one cool guy – has his own rap band. Amir and his brothers. Bob and his partner Ian. And Chris, of course, and the other guys from college.

There's a brilliant party scene in that Audrey Hepburn movie – the one where she lives with that cat – and all the guests are huddled together in a flat and there's unlimited booze and people fall over and it's all completely mad.

My party's going to be something like that.

LIZ'S DIARY

Sunday 26th August

Tenth entry

Some things are never meant to be.

I was beginning to think that maybe the skies were clearing for me and Jimmy. After that scene in Jaguar, I thought he'd never speak to me again as long as I lived, but in fact on the Tuesday, when we were both at work, he attempted a smile. It was a peace offering, and we began to talk again. It turned out that once he'd got over my revelations about Sophie – once I'd made him face the truth – he began to see it was for the best. He had dumped her pretty much immediately after I had told him. I was glad – not on my own account but because he was better off without her.

But here's the funny thing. The very next day Sophie rang me at home for a chat. She told me *she'd* decided to finish with Jimmy. The romance with this Mark-guy was hotting up, she was going to visit him, and Jimmy, for all his new-found wealthy dad and swanky apartment, really wasn't in her league. It was a moment of madness, her going out with him. Maybe it was the whole Coffee Corp scene she was into, and she'd mistaken Jimmy for the scene, but now it was time for her to move on. She knew I'd understand. Even though she and I were very different. I didn't have her aspirations.

'What aspirations?' I'd asked her sweetly. 'To be the world's biggest bitch?'

'Excuse me?' she replied.

'Oh, come off it, Sophie,' I said. 'You've taken Jimmy for a ride, you'll take this Mark for a ride, but not me. The big love of your life is your own sweet self. Bye!'

And I put the phone down. My heart was thumping, and I did feel a bit sick, to say the truth. But I also felt good, purged, pure and I tingled all over. I only wish Jimmy could have heard what I'd said.

At work all the talk was of Jimmy's party. I have to say I was surprised his dad was letting him have one – seeing as though the flat was rented and new and everything. I thought maybe this was his way of cheering Jimmy up after the Sophie business, and if that was the case, then maybe he was a nicer bloke than I thought.

Jimmy was manic about arranging everything. We were all invited – everyone from Coffee Corp, their partners, their siblings, everyone. Even me. We all got pretty excited about it. We discussed clothes, music – Bob said it was a shame the company had changed its policy about letting the staff take home unsold food at the end of the day.

So the big night arrived. For me it arrived a good couple of hours before I left for Jimmy's. I was concerned about what to wear. I wanted to come over like I hadn't bothered much, but at the same time, I did want to appear devastatingly sexy. This is not an easy look to achieve. I messed up my hair with some ultra-strong wax, then decided I looked like Sonic the Hedgehog, so took it all off and washed my hair again. I tried on a long metallic-effect silvery skirt I once bought, but I just can't hack it in a skirt. I just don't feel free to move properly. So I opted for my black combats. I tried on a variety of tops, but each one looked awkward and didn't sit right. The time ticked by and I got more and more panicky. I threw on an old black vest top with a mock-leather tiny black jacket on top, and then thought about my make-up. Definitely as much eye make-up as I could manage. I piled it on. So I looked like it was all a joke, wearing so much make-up, but of course, it was deadly serious. Because deep down I knew I still hadn't given up on Jimmy. And somehow shovelling on the mascara was my way of both making myself look dead sexy and hiding at the same time. I sprayed a good coating of perfume all over me and went.

I arrived at Jimmy's dad's block of flats the same time as Bob and Ian. It kills me the way they both look so alike. They've been together now for four years, which is pretty good for gay men. We all pressed the intercom, the door buzzed, and we walked into this atrium with all the doors to the apartments along each side. Above us were more galleries with apartments, and the space above was criss-crossed by walkways.

We all three stopped and had a look around.

'Very feng shui,' Ian said.

'I don't know,' I commented. 'It reminds me of a prison.'

Once I'd said it, they agreed I was right. You could just imagine prison officers up there, crossing the walkways, pushing meals through the hatches of the doors along the galleries. Before we had time to joke about it, a door to our left opened, and there was Amir.

'Where've you lot been?' he called to us, a bottle of Coke in his hand.

We went in. My eyes took in that brand-new look of white walls and laminated wooden floors and I thought how unlike a home it seemed. It reminded me more of a hotel. The party was through in the sitting area, and frankly everyone looked a bit squashed. Charlene and JC were on a white leather settee, taking up nearly all the room – JC's a big guy – baggy pants, white vest top stark against his black skin. He is gorgeous and he knows it. Amir and two of his mates were standing in the conservatory thing looking out over the street.

'I love it here, man,' Amir said. He introduced to me to Mo and Sadiq. Mo was a little guy but Sadiq was pretty tasty. Only I wasn't entirely focussed on him. I was watching Jimmy.

Or rather, I was more occupied in trying not to watch Jimmy. I rationed out my glances. When I thought long enough had elapsed, I searched him out. He was in the kitchen, drinking beer, with his mate Chris and a couple of other guys. Or he was in the corridor, welcoming in two girls I didn't know. I wanted to go over and have him to myself for a bit, but I also wanted him to seek me out. Every so often I stepped up to the raised kitchen where the booze was and helped myself to something, more because I wanted to maximise the chances of speaking to him. Jimmy was in jeans and a brown T-shirt I hadn't seen before. What makes him really attractive, though, isn't his body – which is pretty fit – but it's his eyes. The way they take in everything and show his every feeling. Like a camera.

There was one point early on when I glanced at him and found he was looking at me. We each began to smile slowly. But then someone else rang on the intercom and Jimmy was pushed out into the corridor to pick up the phone.

JC went over to see to the music. This meant there was a place next to Charlene and I took it. I told her how amazing she looked and she laughed at me. She told me I didn't look too bad myself. She asked me how things were with Maggie and her boyfriend.

'Great,' I told her. 'He's turning out to be a really ace bloke.'

'So when's he moving in?' she grinned at me.

Her question gave me a mild shock.

'I don't know. No one's spoken about it for ages.'

'What are they waiting for?'

'Me, I suppose.'

Charlene laughed. 'Then get a move on, honey. Your mum's no spring chicken. When you're older, you're kind of in a hurry.'

I laughed too, but in an embarrassed way. Charlene had made me feel uncomfortable. Had I still not come to terms with Maggie and Peter? Until this moment, I believed I'd shelved the issue of Peter moving in only because his assignment in Belton had taken priority. He'd explained the best way forward was for him to try to get accepted by the guys he

176

thought were causing the trouble. He said they had cells – none were official, none were affiliated with the party in the election – but they existed nonetheless. That was where the plans were made, where the trouble started. All in secret. Racists, he told us, are essentially cowards, they work underhand, they only attack in big enough numbers – I thought of that football match where thousands of racist supporters chanted insults at the one black footballer out there on the pitch and I felt myself swell with anger. Not the appropriate mood for a party. So I turned my gaze to what was going on around me.

I was quiet, watching Bob and Ian dancing a bit, and Amir rifling through the DVD collection by the telly. It didn't work. I wondered what Peter was doing now, and hoped he would be safe. I was glad he had Maggie and me.

I banished all those sober thoughts by springing to my feet and joining Bob and Ian in the middle of the floor dancing to Diana Ross. Ian was a great dancer but frankly Bob has two left feet and I told him so.

'OK,' he said. 'You're on clean-round duty tomorrow. All day.'

We got some more to drink and chatted a while. When Charlene and JC hit the floor, we all stopped to watch them. Then we all drank and danced even more. The party was taking off. It was so hot someone opened all the windows out onto the street. Jimmy said it didn't matter about the noise as there was a club over the road that was belting out sounds. Amir's mate Mo put on some Bhangra. Everyone was moving now, and I was thinking, this is my kind of party, everyone into it, all of us together. Just then I felt one hundred per cent alive – utterly myself, but also part of everyone else. We were all one big party animal.

Then Jimmy started to dance next to me. I was suddenly totally conscious of myself again. I was an isolated individual. I saw what my legs and arms were doing. I felt myself slowing down. My heart was pounding only I wasn't sure if it was from the dancing or my emotions. The record drew to a close. Everyone whooped with delight.

'Do you wanna see round the flat?' Jimmy asked me.

'Why not?' I said.

We broke away. He made some unnecessary comments about the room we were in and the kitchen. But to tell you the truth, I wasn't that interested. I said to him, 'This could be anywhere. It doesn't have anyone's personality in it. I don't get a feel of what your dad is like.'

'Yeah,' he said. An uncertain look crossed his face. I picked up on that. I felt myself leaving the party in my head and being there right next to Jimmy in his private space. 'Are you getting to like him – your dad?' I persisted.

'Yeah. But my mum says . . . says he was no good.'

'Really?'

'But that was a long time ago. I reckon he's changed since then.'

I said, 'You're right. And a marriage is made of two people. Maybe your mum brought out the wrong side of him.' Jimmy looked grateful, glad I'd said that.

Some R & B started up. Jimmy and I went out in the corridor where it was quieter.

'I get on well with my dad,' he said. 'I think he's good for me.'

Then he said, 'You are too.'

He really said those words. They made my knees go weak. I grinned at him, stupidly happy. He reached out and took my hand. Really.

'I'll show you the rest of the flat. That's the bathroom,' he said, which was silly, as the door was open and I could see it was the bathroom. I giggled.

'And this is my room. We can get away from the others for a while.' I agreed, but my voice was small and nervous. I swallowed hard. Jimmy opened the door and there, on his bed, were Bob and Ian, just snogging, but still – there was no room for us.

There was a door at right angles to his room, and Jimmy opened that.

'Come in here,' he said.

I could see immediately it was his dad's room. I surveyed it rapidly.

'Omigod,' I said. 'There's a connecting door with your room!'

'Yeah. The whole wall is removable, so you could use the place as a one-bedroom flat.'

I thought, I would hate that.

Jimmy sat on the bed, and I perched by him. For some reason, that feeling of lust I had before had ebbed away. Parents do that to you, don't they? Turn you into sexless creatures. I sensed that Jimmy, too, had cooled. Still, he put an arm around me. My eyes flicked round the room, looking for signs of his dad, a trail of his presence. But the white fitted wardrobe doors weren't telling any tales. On his bedside table was a book, however. Black leather binding. Gold lettering on the front. *The Fellowship of Albion.* I frowned to myself, trying to work out what that was. Some novel like *Lord of the Rings?* Only it looked like a very short book.

Jimmy said, 'I want to try something.'

'What?' I asked.

And the next thing was, he kissed me. For a split second I was shocked. Then as I grew into the kiss, felt the softness of his lips and his tongue finding its way to electrify mine, my body turned to milk and honey. The kiss released sensations that rippled frighteningly through my body. There was one moment of hesitation as I wondered if I ought to give myself up to this? And just as I decided to go with it and damn the consequences I felt Jimmy freeze. There was some sort of commotion in the hallway. Next thing, Amir opened the bedroom door and I saw him announce nervously, 'Your dad's arrived.'

Jimmy shot up off the bed. I was thinking, if he likes his dad so much, and thinks he's such a great guy, why's he so scared? And at the same time I wanted him back with me again. Just that one kiss had turned me into only half a person. I needed Jimmy back so I could find my whole self again.

But I also got up off the bed and followed Jimmy and Amir back into the sitting area.

There was his dad, in smart trousers and a blazer, looking around him, taking in the whole of the party – Charlene and

JC sprawled on the settee, Dr Dre on the stereo, Sadiq wrapped round one of the girls in the conservatory, Chris snogging another girl, cans of lager everywhere. And just then Bob and Ian returned, Bob's arm round Ian's shoulder. I watched Jimmy's dad, to see what he made of it all. I watched Jimmy too.

The conversation died away. People let go of each other. Jimmy's dad's face was entirely impassive. I saw a muscle jump in his cheek. I was expecting a torrent of anger, though, to be honest, we'd not made a mess. Nothing had been spilled. The windows were open so there was no smoke anywhere. Nothing was going on that wouldn't go on at anyone's party. Less, in fact. But I got the sense that Jimmy's dad was fighting something inside him. There was a struggle going on deep down. I felt myself clench too, with the suspense of it.

Jimmy had his eyes trained on his dad. This moment, in which everyone was waiting for a reaction from him, must have lasted all of five seconds. Five very long seconds. At then end, he just said heavily:

'I think it's late, now, don't you?'

Amir approached him. 'Sorry, Mr ...' He realised he wasn't sure of Jimmy's dad's last name. 'Nice to meet you.'

He thrust out his hand. Jimmy's dad didn't respond. That was rude. Maybe I imagined this bit, but there was a momentary look of loathing in his eyes. I didn't get it. Amir is the most likeable bloke you could ever meet. Jimmy's dad just said, 'The party's over.'

I looked at Jimmy then, to see how he would take that.

181

If it was me, I'd have said, well, fine, so how it about it, everyone, let's go on somewhere else. But Jimmy didn't. I guess things were still so new with his dad he didn't want to risk upsetting him. Like when you're ten years old or something and your parents are still gods. When it's much too terrifying to ever think of standing up for yourself. When you're a professional parent-pleaser.

It hit me then that my real rival for Jimmy wasn't Sophie, but his dad. Because the Jimmy who had kissed me on his dad's bed had vanished, as if he had never been. The Jimmy who was standing in front of me now had linked himself in some strange way to the middle-aged man stock-still in the middle of this room, who was making us all feel like scum.

'Anyone want to stay and help me clear round?' Jimmy asked.

His dad cut in. 'No need. We can do it together.'

'I'll stay,' I said. I felt my heels dig into the carpet. I didn't understand why I was doing this.

Then Jimmy's dad locked eyes with me. Those weren't Jimmy's eyes. Oh – I'm not saying he's not really Jimmy's dad – they have the same bone structure, the same chin, their hair falls in the same way. But Jimmy's dad was an entirely different animal to him, and I didn't like him one bit. He filled me with a deep revulsion. It even sickened me that I'd sat on his bed.

One by one everyone left. They all thanked Jimmy, said it was a great party. I stayed put.

'I'll do the washing-up,' I said brightly.

Jimmy's dad said, 'We have a dishwasher.'

I ignored him. I began to pick up cans and bowls that once had crisps in and took them to the kitchen. Jimmy followed me, then whispered that I had better go too. He said he'd text.

'What's the problem?' I asked him. 'You could do with an extra pair of hands.'

'Liz,' he said, pleadingly.

His dad was watching us and that spooked me. Even then, I hastily whispered to Jimmy, 'I get the feeling he's not too pleased with you. I'm hanging round so he doesn't go ballistic at you.'

'I can handle him, Liz.'

'So you don't want me,' I replied.

Jimmy didn't have time to reply.

'Do you have a coat?' Jimmy's dad asked me. His voice alone was edging me out. It was stolid and coldly polite. Jimmy was looking down at the floor.

'Don't have a go at Jimmy,' I said desperately. 'We were just having fun.'

'Nice to meet you,' he said.

I backed out, hoping against hope that Jimmy would follow me, but knowing that he wouldn't. In a moment I was out in the atrium. The jail door banged shut.

I got a taxi back home. I held my phone in my hands, waiting for the text that would assure me that Jimmy was OK. None arrived. Then I told myself off for being such an idiot. So what if Jimmy's dad read him the riot act? All parents do that occasionally. But then, if Maggie had come home and found me having that sort of party, she'd have joined in. Someone would have poured her a drink and she'd have found one of my friends to chat up.

In between wanting Jimmy again, and fearing for him, there was no rest for me last night.

JIMMY

We're surrounded by all the party debris, facing each other. *Shoot-out at the OK Corral.*

Then my dad's face relaxes. He runs his hand through his hair. 'Looks like you had some night,' he tells me.

'Er . . . yeah.'

'It's probably a good idea if we clean up before we go to bed.'

I watch him begin to pick stuff up. I realise I'm stone cold sober, because I was expecting him to half kill me. But as I go round the flat taking paper cups to the kitchen, I realise how wrong I was. I was expecting trouble from him because of what my mum told me. Her weird story has affected me – but as I keep telling myself, that was then and this is now.

'These friends of yours,' my dad says. 'They're mainly from your coffee shop.'

'Yeah, except for Chris and the people he brought with him.'

'Friends of circumstance. I should imagine they're not really your sort.'

'I don't know. I—'

'You can't really have a lot in common with them.'

I think about that. There was some truth in what he's

185

saying. We didn't choose to be friends, but now we are . . . I'm too tired to start making sense of this. I let my dad do the talking.

'When all's said and done, it's best to stick to your own kind. Your own kind will always look out for you. Where there are conflicting interests, that's when problems occur.'

I pick up someone's crumpled-up tissue.

'That girl,' my dad goes. 'The one who wouldn't go at the end. She's also from your coffee shop?'

'Liz,' I say, and as I speak her name the memory of kissing her floods over me. The feeling is so powerful I stop what I'm doing. I didn't even plan it, I didn't even know it was going to happen. But watching her dance made me feel as if I had to get her alone. Once I had her alone, then I just had to kiss her. And once I was kissing her – I still can't quite believe it – me and Liz! It's dawning on me now that I fancy her a hundred times more than I ever did Sophie, who was just eye-candy. All show. But Liz – she's real. And where are we now? What does that kiss mean? Are we going out together? Or will she hate me for making a pass at her? Does she really fancy me?

'Liz,' Dad says thoughtfully. 'She's English, presumably.'

I shrug. I'd never thought about it.

'Still, I wouldn't see too much of her, if I was you.'

'Why?'

'I know that type. She seems a very angry girl to me – a troublemaker. She's not very feminine, either.'

'I don't know about that,' I say, a bit surprised and disappointed that Dad has taken against Liz.

186

'She strikes me as being rather strange. I didn't like the way she was looking at you. Like she has some kind of obsession with you. You noticed how she wouldn't leave. I had to force her. That kind of girl has difficulty forming normal relationships with boys, and I should imagine she's fixed on you and has developed a fantasy around you. Keep away from her, Jimmy.'

'But I—'

'How are you fixed tomorrow?' Dad goes on. 'Are you going in to work?'

'No. Bob—'

'Good. I've decided that if you're seriously interested in film, you need to have your own camcorder. You have to start somewhere. All the best directors begin young. I thought we'd go out in the afternoon and look at the shops.'

'A camcorder!' I repeat in disbelief. The times I'd begged Mum for one! And now it might really happen . . .

My dad beams at me. 'I think so. And then I was wondering . . . in the evening . . . whether you'd like to come with me and meet some of my friends. We're meeting down in Belton.'

'Yeah. Nice one.' What else can I say?

'Looks like we've nearly finished,' Dad comments pleasantly. 'I won't clean the floor till the morning. Those two men who came in at the end. They're not . . .'

'Gay? Yeah. That's Bob and his partner Ian.'

Dad shakes his head ruefully. Well, I'm not surprised. His generation isn't as broad-minded as ours. And it's a relief to me to find out he's not all perfect. I don't push the issue with Bob.

187

So we turn in for the night. I lie in bed and discover that I'm not at all tired. I can hear Dad next door getting ready for the night, I hear the faint groan of his mattress as he eases himself into bed. I see the door between us and think of what Liz said – how she wouldn't like to be so close to him.

I don't know what to do about Liz. I'm not sure what my dad says is true, but I don't want to be in a position where I'm confronting him with a girlfriend that he doesn't like. Not at the moment, anyway. And since even *I* don't know what I want to happen here, the best thing is that I ease off for now. I remember I promised to text her, but I decide not to. Because right now it would seem disloyal to Dad. A camcorder! That is amazing! I have this idea for a short – about a haunted house – I'd like to find some derelict place and shoot entirely without actors (that way it's low budget) and just pick up sounds, shadows and that. So everything is what you imagine and nothing actually happens. So the viewer is making up the picture in his own head. Forget *The Ring* – this will be way scarier!

I can hear my dad turning over pages. He's reading something.

Horror movies work by suggestion – as soon as you see what's frightening you, you can deal with it. It's what you can't see – the thing round the corner that you know is there, but won't reveal itself.

A faint flick as Dad turns off the light above his bed. No more light from underneath the adjoining door. My room is almost entirely dark.

When I close my eyes and try to sleep, I get this feeling as if I'm rushing somewhere without my own permission. I think it's because I had too much to drink. Everything's moving around me and I'm still. I wonder where Liz is – and I feel a bit mean, to tell you the truth, because I know I want her but I'm going to hold off. I think it's better if I stay away from her for now. But that kiss. No harm in reliving it. Not if it helps me get to sleep.

I really am awake now, and it's feeling good.

We're in the car and on our way to Belton. Belton's quite a way out of the city, almost a separate town in itself. A bit old, a bit scazzy. I never go there – why would I want to? We're cruising along a dual carriageway, stopping for traffic lights from time to time, driving past DIY warehouses, supermarkets, motor discount stores. I'm caressing my new camcorder in my mind – mentally examining its sleek silver lines, running through its functions, looking forward to getting home and taking it out of its box again and exploring it thoroughly, reading the handbook, trying out a few shots – I'm so into this that when Dad starts talking I only half listen. Until I realise what it is he's talking about.

'... I used to throw things when I got angry. I did it because I was frightened if I didn't smash something, I'd hit out at *her*. Even at my worst, I knew that was wrong. I hope she didn't tell you I'd ever laid a hand on her, as that would be a downright lie.'

'What? Mum? No,' I stuttered. 'She never said you hit her.'

'Good. But I daresay she told you I locked her in the flat.'

'Yeah.' We're moving along at a steady forty. Little other traffic on the road. I'm concentrating now.

'I did do that, and I can see now it was wrong. But I couldn't work out what else to do. I know she wanted to leave me and take you with her. I'd also begun to think we weren't suited. I didn't know how to persuade her to stay, or how to change if she did stay. I wanted one more chance. So I thought, if I could just keep her in the flat while I went to work . . .'

He indicates left, then stops for the lights. I'm beginning to see there are two versions of everything. Different angles. It all depends where you're looking from.

'It was a stupid thing to do – the action of an ignorant, desperate young man. I bitterly regret it. I'm hoping that one day she'll let me apologise and we can start afresh.'

I think I'd better tell him. 'She's very settled with Steve.'

'I know. I can see that. I accept I've lost her.' Then he smiles. 'But I've found you.'

We move off again. I'm wondering now who these friends are we're meeting. Dad's told me very little about them.

'Jimmy,' Dad continues, 'I want to try to explain to you how I changed – because I have changed. And these chaps you're meeting tonight – they're a very important part of it.'

'Yeah?'

'I started going to meetings just after I left the army. I stopped when I was in Cyprus. But when I came back to England, I got more involved. You see, you have to look back at why I behaved so badly to your mother. I never had much of an education, as you know. Society was in breakdown back then. All those teachers and all their liberal values. Just letting the kids get on with it, allowing them to do their own thing. Even if that 'own thing' was failing. We had no structure, no discipline. No wonder I was angry, no wonder I didn't know how to control myself.'

'Then you joined the army,' I prompted him. 'After you and Mum split.'

'I did. And it gave me the discipline I needed. But that was only the beginning. I was beginning to think about why the system had failed me. After my father died I was brought up by my mother, and she couldn't handle me. It wasn't her fault. A mere woman can't control a wild boy. And all around us society was in meltdown – there were riots in the streets – black, white, all mixed up. A society gone to seed. We'd lost whatever we had that made us great. I didn't know who I was, Jimmy.'

I'm listening and working out that my dad must have been a kid in the early 1980s. What movies were out then? I'm racking my brains. *Raiders of the Lost Ark*. *Chariots of Fire*. Films about heroes. I guess he wanted to be a hero and he was frustrated to find he wasn't.

I ask him, 'Did you see *Chariots of Fire* when it first came out?'

'Yes!' he announces and smiles. 'Now that was a great film!' Momentarily he glances at me and I see his face is lit up with approval. I must have said the right thing. Good.

'I want you to meet my friends, Jimmy, as they're the ones who've given me the support I've needed. They've given me

191

direction. A man needs to have other men around him – a brotherhood.'

'Yeah!' I'm trying to chime in with the way my dad's mind is working. I'm slightly lost, but I get the feeling it's important to stay on his wavelength. 'Like in *Lord of the Rings*. The fellowship. Nine of them all sticking by each other.'

'Fellowship – that's exactly it! Jimmy – I know you'll fit in.'

'Fellowship,' I carry on, glad to be pleasing him. 'Even though those guys were dwarves and elves and hobbits – I mean – I read that Tolkien based all of that stuff on old legends about knights in Anglo-Saxon times and rings being a sign of loyalty, and . . .'

I didn't really know what I was on about, but I've always liked saying the kind of things that make other people happy. My dad was grinning from ear to ear. Maybe he's a Tolkien fan.

And finally we turn into the car park of an old, dilapidated pub. The Georgian Arms. A shabby Victorian pile of red bricks that need repointing. Not the sort of joint I'd normally be seen in. I'm weighing up how much to drink as I put away quite a bit last night. We get out, Dad locks the car and I follow him up a few stone steps to a short hallway with rooms leading off. We enter the lounge bar where there's Sky Sport on a huge screen and a central bar with optics gleaming. At the back are a flight of steps. Dad nods at the barman who greets him by name. Then Dad ascends the stairs, with me in tow. The carpet has a dark red background, a floral design, and it's slightly threadbare. I smell stale cigarette smoke, the tang of beer. Someone scores a goal downstairs and cheers erupt.

We're upstairs now and on the landing. A door on our left is slightly ajar and Dad pushes it fully open. We're in an oblong room with several rows of chairs set out in a semi-circle, facing a table with two chairs behind it. The grimy window tries and fails to look out onto the car park. There's a massive, dusty chandelier hanging down from the ceiling. There are portraits on the wall of old guys. And just then some people walk in, talking as they come.

'Mike!' one of them says as he enters. Then, looking at me, 'And this must be Jimmy!'

They're all shaking my hand. More blokes arrive. I think in the end there are about ten of them. A couple are quite old – silver-haired, someone's granddads. Then there are three guys just a little older than me – very smart – I'm worried we're all Jehovah's Witnesses or something. But I relax. I see they're carrying pints in with them, so that's OK, then. Then a fat geezer comes in with another, younger man. Short. Hairy arms. He looks a bit nervous – like me.

But most of the guys here are around my dad's age. There's a good feeling in the room. You sense these people like each other. Now I'm getting curious what this meeting is all about, and I'm kind of glad my dad hasn't told me. I enjoy the mystery element. I know it's got something to do with a fellowship, and I'm wondering whether they play Dungeons and Dragons. No. Not likely.

One of the blokes, immaculately dressed in a fawn sweater over chinos, takes the seat behind the table and calls the

193

meeting to order. Then they do all that boring stuff about minutes of the last meeting and signing them correct and apologies for absence. No one else talks. They all look serious. I get it now. They're like Freemasons – that lot who have a secret society and help each other in business and have weird rituals. Cool.

The man behind the table introduces himself as Norman and then he welcomes me and the other guy I noticed – the short one. He says he's glad to have us show an interest, and so he'll take a moment to explain to us what the Fellowship of Albion is all about.

I listen carefully, keen to pick up the rules.

'Tradition,' he goes. Then he repeats it once more. 'Tradition. That's what links us to each other. It's like an unbroken line that goes from generation to generation – father to son.' I see my dad glance at me. We smile at each other. 'It's by remembering the past that we find out who we truly are. So who are we?

'We're English. England is our mother country. We come from the Celts, the Angles, the Saxons – and there may even be a bit of Viking blood in there. All those tribes came together to form the race we call the English – England – the country that more than any other has shaped world history. The land of Shakespeare and Milton – of Constable and Turner – of a race of Kings and Queens that the world envies. The English – who discovered the rest of the world, colonised America, enriched India, brought civilisation to Africa. A land of fair play and above all, freedom. A land of tradition, restraint and order. A land of village greens, of family values, of fairness, of pride. Of national pride.

'National pride – those are two dirty words these days. But why should they be? To be proud of your country is to be proud of your brothers and sisters – your fellow citizens. It's to be proud of your traditions, of the mother and father that brought you up, to those who died in two World Wars so we should prosper today. England is your mother and father both. Be proud of them. Make your country proud of you!'

I'm feeling quite stirred by all of this. I glance quickly at the other newcomer. I see his eyes are trained on Norman, drinking in his every word.

'National pride is politically incorrect. That's what some people would have us believe. Those people who want to mix us all up together, who want to give our hard-earned pennies to economic migrants – or to give them another name, scroungers – who come here fed up with conditions in their own countries to live off *our* welfare state, fought for by *your* fathers and grandfathers. Filthy scum with their fundamentalist religions and bringing in terrorists with them.

'Did you know – a whistle-blower in Belton council found out that there was a family of fifteen Pakistanis living in a three-bedroomed council house and do you want to know how much in benefits that family brought home every week? More than an English pensioner gets in eight weeks. *And* the father was moonlighting as a mini-cab driver. And that's only one family that we know about. How many more of them are defrauding this country, eating away at our resources, putting nothing back?

'More than that – our culture is being eaten away. Like

chalk cliffs, fragments of Britain are falling into the sea. Try to find a traditional English chippy – it's all curry houses and Chinese takeaways. Our children are listening to negro music, watching Bollywood movies. Our kids are confused – they don't know who they are any more. That's why they turn to drugs and violence. We've got to save our own kids!

'That's what the Fellowship of Albion is all about. We're not a political party. We're not exactly a pressure group. Instead we defend the English way of life however we can. We take what action is appropriate. We depend on our individual members to . . .'

I am sitting stock-still in my seat not daring to move. I'm cold with fear. This is not the Freemasons. This is not some nerdy bunch of old blokes playing games. I have walked right into some kind of crypto-fascist, right-wing, racist cell. No – correction – I've been taken here. By my dad. Who is clearly part of this. I don't want to believe this is all happening, but I've got to. It's real, and I'm really in it.

I don't want to give anything away. I'm staring straight ahead, thinking about what I've just heard. These are my mates that Norman's been talking about – that's Amir and Charlene and JC. I've never thought about it properly before, but those people – and Liz – and Bob and everyone – they're my people. Pennies are dropping so quickly now, clattering in my head. When my dad came home after the party, it wasn't the mess that he was stressed about – it was my friends – the ones he said I had nothing in common with.

Why hadn't Mum said anything? Probably because she didn't know. I think back over what Dad had told me, and work out he got involved with all of this after he left her. I shoot a glance at him now. He's absorbed in the meeting. My eyes scan the room. The other new guy looks as nervous as me – or maybe that's just my imagination, because I don't want to feel on my own here. I swallow hard. I remember how I dismissed Liz when she went ballistic at those three kids, and I feel guilty. I can feel beads of sweat on my forehead.

But the worst thing is, I don't know what to do.

By rights I should stand up now and tell everyone there's been a huge mistake. I shouldn't be here. I don't like what they stand for. I should call them all bastards to their faces, and tell my dad I'll make my own way home – to Carol's.

But I don't. I'm still sitting here, thinking about it.

Someone's said something that merits a round of applause. There's clapping. I don't join in. Somebody's saying something about a September festival a week before the by-election, a festival in Belton's Hillside district, the one where there's a huge new mosque that won a civic award recently. There's going to be a further meeting about that.

I think maybe the best thing to do would be to say nothing until this meeting is over, then tell my dad I want nothing more to do with this outfit. Yeah.

I'd never even properly thought about racism before. Why should I? I'm just a film nut. I don't deal in the real world. So I'm at a loss now. My dad seems unaware of how I feel. I don't understand how he could have thought I'd be up for a group like this. But what if. . . what if he sees me as impressionable, without a mind of my own. I never hesitated when he came into my life and took control. He thinks I'm a pushover. He thinks I'm his – his son. His property.

I'm sitting here, and it's like I'm being propelled at the speed of light through a second adolescence. I realise I don't want to be like my dad. I don't want to be anything like my dad. Only I don't know how to break away. I don't know when to do it – how to do it – and hell, I don't even know if I want to – because he's my dad. Can you ever break away completely from your dad? Should you?

Everyone stands. They start singing – Blake's 'Jerusalem' followed by the National Anthem. I couldn't join in even if I wanted to because my mouth is dry as dust. And then the meeting's over and the men cluster in groups making comments. Norman brings over this short bloke and introduces him as Dennis. We shake hands limply.

Then my first, feeble protest. 'Dad,' I say, 'I think I'd like to go home.'

Dad looks a bit disappointed but seems not to suspect anything. I keep my head down, stare at my trainers, take gulps of air as we reach the car park. Get into the passenger seat of the car. My dad feels like an alien to me now.

'Well,' he says to me. 'What did you think?'

'I'm not sure,' I say, feeling my way.

'Jimmy – I can't tell you how much I owe to the Fellowship. It was through Norman I got my job in Iraq – and after Colin was murdered, they helped me through it. They've set me up here and are paying the rent for the apartment – George organised that. He was at the meeting but I didn't have a chance to introduce you. He's a property agent and looks after the block. They're all good men, Jimmy. Brothers.'

'But they're racists.' I feel better now I've said this. Dad glances quickly at me, suddenly alert.

'Racist? In the pure sense of the word, yes, they are. They believe in the purity of our own race. What we say is not that any one race is better than another, but they should all be kept separate. How is that racist?'

I couldn't answer him. It's the same with some of the teachers at school – you know they're going to have an answer for everything, so you don't bother. Only I do say:

'Amir's my mate, and he's OK.'

My dad says, 'After the party, I noticed a vile smell in the bathroom.'

Now I want to get out of the car but we're halfway between Belton and the city. Instead I stop talking. I hope he notices I'm annoyed. I watch him switch on the radio.

I wonder if I can go home tonight? I know Mum won't mind. But it's already half ten and they'll be on their way to bed. Better to stick it out just one more night. It's not as if I'm in any danger. I might even try to have it out with Dad, to try and explain to him why he's so wrong. Since he loves me so much, maybe he'll listen to me. I'm back scripting something in my head now, a happy ending where Dad sees the error of his ways. Because he never had the benefit of a son, no one had ever pointed out to him that the world has moved on since the Dark Ages. We can have a final, emotional scene with the camera darting back and forth between us, when I teach my dad about racial harmony. Hell, I'll even get Amir round to rustle us up a chicken madras!

LIZ'S DIARY

Sunday 26th August, continued

Eleventh entry

Dennis! I said to Peter, if you were going undercover you could have come up with a cooler name. You could have been Josh or Zak or something. 'Or Che Guevara', Maggie joked. 'That way they would have never guessed at his true identity.'

We were all laughing, only the situation wasn't funny. Not at all funny. I'll go back and explain.

Maggie and I were on our way to bed when someone rang repeatedly at the doorbell. My heart started pounding. I sensed immediately it was trouble.

I stood behind Maggie as she opened the door – and Peter was there. Peter – with a gash over his eye, blood on his shirt and dirt on his clothes. Maggie stifled a scream and we pulled him in.

'What happened to you?' I shouted at him.

Maggie was beside herself, examining his wounds, asking him over and again if he was all right.

'What happened?' I shouted louder.

'I was beaten up,' Peter explained. 'But I'm OK. It's just

my eye, I think. And where they winded me. Honestly, I'll survive.'

'We ought to go to the hospital,' Maggie said.

'Who beat you up?' I asked.

'Those guys from the Fellowship of Albion.'

'The *what?*' Maggie exclaimed. 'Liz – don't just stand there – go and get Peter something. Some whisky. A cup of tea. Look, he's shaking!' She sat him down and knelt by him. I left them to put the kettle on.

I padded into the kitchen in my dressing gown and bare feet. The Fellowship of Albion. That was so familiar. Only I didn't have the opportunity to think where I'd heard of that name. I switched on the kettle and returned to the lounge so I could hear Peter's explanation of what happened.

'It was after the meeting. I thought I'd convinced them I was genuine. I don't know what it was I said that gave me away. It must have been afterwards, when we were having a drink together. I don't know.'

'What meeting?' we both asked.

In the distance I heard the kettle click 'off' and ran into the kitchen to make his tea. When I came back I caught the tail end of his explanation to Maggie.

'. . . to try to do something at the community festival in Belton. They were proper fascists. Banging on about racial supremacy. Only I didn't have a tape recorder with me and I could hardly sit there taking notes. I was careful not to have anything with me which would— Maybe it was when I took out my wallet to pay for the drinks – were my business cards in there?'

He was still in a state of shock. His hands were trembling as he accepted the tea. I stole a glance at Maggie and there were tears in her eyes. She hardly ever cries.

'He's a hero!' I declared. 'I think it takes guts to do what you've done. So is this group the one spreading all the rumours, causing that harassment? Amir's been telling me about the trouble they're having – he lives in Belton.'

'I'm pretty sure they are. That's what they do – provoke attacks, get other people to do their dirty work. They're cowards. Hell, it took two of them to do me over!' He laughed then, and so did I. It was a relief to be able to laugh.

'I think it's amazing that you infiltrated them? Did you use your real name?'

Which was when he said he was called Dennis. And we all laughed some more, even Maggie, and that broke the tension. Then she sprang up, went to the kitchen, and got a packet of frozen peas out of the freezer, and told Peter to hold it over his eye to help with the swelling. Yes – there was Peter sitting on our settee with a packet of Birds' Eye frozen peas on his face. I felt giggly – but also shaken – and scared. Peter couldn't stop talking. It was his way of dealing with what had happened.

'They were mostly middle-aged guys – they didn't look like thugs. More like ex-army types, all ramrod straight in their chairs. And one young bloke – about your age, Liz. I didn't like that – it shows they're getting their message across, they're gaining supporters. And they make it all sound so reasonable, what they say. I'm sure I didn't give anything away. It was afterwards – did one of my cards fall out of my wallet? – someone jostled me – I don't remember. Then when I said my goodbyes and went out into the car park, two guys came from nowhere and went for me. And threatened me with worse – unless I kept my mouth shut.'

'Oh my God!' Maggie said. 'Tell the police. Because you know who they are.'

'But I don't. They weren't the same blokes from the meeting. But from what they called me, I know they're the same crowd.'

'What did they call you?' I asked.

'Forget it,' Peter said. 'Let's just say they know I'm not one of them.'

'I still think we should go to casualty,' Maggie insisted.

'No – I'll be fine,' Peter said. 'Hell, the worst of it is that my cover's blown. The investigation's dead. And it makes me furious with myself because this is something I care about. If ever I wanted to come through on a story, this is the one.'

'I think it must be so hard to be convincing when you have views exactly the opposite to other people. I could never, ever pretend to be racist,' I told him. I wanted to make him feel better.

'No, you couldn't,' Maggie agreed. 'You've never been able to hide anything.'

Mum was right, but just then I was more focussed on Peter. I felt so sorry for him. I wanted to do something to make him feel better. And I admired enormously what he was trying to do. So this is what I said:

'Why don't you stay the night?'

Both Maggie and Peter looked at me, surprised.

'Unless you needed to get back for any reason,' I added. 'Because it's no big deal. You can stay here whenever.'

'Thanks, Liz,' Maggie said meaningfully.

'Yeah . . . thanks,' Peter stumbled.

And I thought to myself, you ought to thank me, because I've just given you the biggest present anyone could give. My mum. I can't pretend there wasn't a pang as I did it. I knew *I* was letting *her* go, whereas normally it's parents who let kids go – to university or wherever. But you can't cling to your mum for ever. That's not natural either.

'So what's going to happen now? Is there *any* way you can carry on with the investigation?'

Peter shook his head. 'And I'll have to report back to the paper. It doesn't look good. For anyone.'

Writing all this down helps to put my own problems into proportion. Here's Peter trying to head off a riot and getting done over, and I've spent the whole of the day stressing about some boy, worrying whether he meant his kiss or not, and trying to decide if we have a future. What a loser I am! But as much as I despise myself, I still can't help thinking back to that kiss in his dad's bedroom, and . . .

I remember where I saw those words – The Fellowship of Albion. It was the lettering on that book on his dad's bedside table.

So . . . Jimmy's *dad* is part of that group?

I've just had a think about it. He must be. Everything is beginning to make sense to me, but the sense it makes is so horrible I find myself resisting it. That's why his dad was so spooked when he saw all of Jimmy's mates, the Coffee Corp crew. Asians, blacks, gays, the lot.

But if Jimmy's dad *is* in that fellowship thing, do I tell Jimmy? Would he believe me if I did? Will he listen to me if I start badmouthing his dad?

I have no choice but to find out, because Jimmy has to know what I know. And for the first time in my life, I'm really scared.

JIMMY

Cheese and ham panini! On automatic, I reach into the display cabinet, get one out, slam it on the chopping board, slice it in half, toss it into the grill, push down the lid and stand there as the red digits count down.

And I carry on thinking. So far I've worked out that it's not fair just to walk out on my dad without giving him a reason. So I'll have to tell him that his politics stink. Yeah, I'm still tempted to try to put him straight and explain that racism is wrong and that maybe he didn't realise what he was getting himself into. Maybe now he's got me I can save him from the mess he's got himself into. Lone ranger Jimmy.

I can feel the heat coming off from the panini grill. *Beep, beep, beep.* I fling it open and realise I've grilled a cheese panini – not a shred of ham in sight. When no one's looking I throw it in the bin and get another. Another glance round to see I'm not discovered, and I notice Liz is eyeing me. Again.

She's been like that all morning. Attentive, watchful – and if it wasn't for the fact I'm giving myself a headache here trying to work out what to say to my dad and when to say it and whether to say it at all or just wait for a bit or go and talk to Mum except she'd say I told you so, or—

'You OK, Jimmy?' Liz asks me.

I try to grin at her and pretend everything's shipshape. She's acting weird. I can feel her concern for me edging me into a corner. And Bob is also watching me. Liz returns her attention to the till and now I'm wondering what's eating her and ignore the beeping of the panini grill until Bob reminds me.

'I think you've given me the wrong change,' Liz's customer says to her, very nicely.

I don't ever remember Liz doing that before. I watch her, flustered, unlock the till and sort it out. Bob's noticed that too. I turn to read the notices on the filter coffee machine. *Remove basket slowly. May contain hot liquid. Handle with care.* When we got home last night Dad suggested we investigate the camcorder and so I got it out of the box and held it in my hand. I slipped my right hand up and under the strap and held that compact silver machine in the palm of my hand. With my thumb I could switch it on and off. My index fingers worked the zoom button. You can see what you're filming on the flip-out screen. That was why I didn't say anything to Dad last night. I was too busy with the camcorder.

'Jimmy,' Bob said warningly. 'You were asked for a latte and cappuccino.'

I apologise profusely and am aware again of Liz keeping an eye on me. Then Bob tells her he'll take over on the till and she should go and collect some empties. She shoots me a meaningful glance and fetches the tray from the back room.

It throws me when Amir struts into the shop, beaming

208

from ear to ear, and walks straight behind the bar. He isn't supposed to be in today. Bob says exactly the same thing to him and Amir looks surprised.

'No way, man!' he says. 'I thought it was Tuesday!'

Bob laughs. 'Still only Monday, last time I checked. Seems like all my staff are suffering from mass distraction. Could it be a hangover from Jimmy's party?'

'I didn't have that much to drink,' I argue. 'Give me a break.'

Then Bob flicks his eyes at Liz, then at me. 'There are other sorts of hangovers,' he says. 'Know what I mean?'

I didn't, but Amir guffaws.

Bob clasps his hand on my shoulder. 'Listen, mate. I saw what you were up to with Liz. And I think you need to sort it all out. Seeing as though Amir's in by accident, and Charlene'll be along soon, why don't you two have an extended lunch hour and talk it all through?'

Liz looks as confused as me.

'Here at Coffee Corp, we all like happy endings,' Bob mugged.

I got it then. He was trying to get Liz and me together. I smile despite myself because here was Bob playing Cupid while I'm totally stressed about my dad. And Liz is staring at me like I've got the plague. I even remember what my dad said about her being obsessed with me.

But that thought only lasts a split second. Because now I'm thinking the one person I can talk to about this whole mess is Liz. And that Bob has done me a favour, even though it's not the one he thinks he's done. I notice Liz is taking off her apron and preparing for our break seemingly unembarrassed by Bob's teasing and Amir's sniggers.

Once we're out on the street, she says, 'We can go to the art gallery.'

There's a café there, and it's as good a place as any to have a talk. It's about a ten-minute walk away, and all that time – all that time – neither of us says a word. I wonder what she's thinking. I even wonder what I'm thinking. Because now I'm with her again thoughts of my dad are dissolving and I'm only conscious of Liz walking by me, me and Liz alone together in the city. I'd like to put my arm round her but guess this would not be a good thing to do. She's preoccupied and an instinct tells me it hasn't got anything to do with our kiss at my party. Liz isn't the kind of girl who plays games. Now I'm worried that there's something wrong in her life – because – if there was – she could count on me for support.

I sort of hope there is – I feel like being the hero for once.

We walk up the steps of the art gallery advertising its current exhibition of Pre-Raphaelites, whatever they are. But the soulful eyes of the woman on the poster remind me of Liz.

She leads me into the café which is through a corridor on our right. It's a large space with windows on two sides. There aren't too many people around the pale wooden tables – some middle-aged people reading books, a mother with a baby in a stroller. We don't even bother to get drinks but sit down at a small round table in a corner. Between us there's a solitary plastic flower keeling over in a glass vase and a metal container of serviettes. Someone's not cleaned the table properly – I can see the faint ring of a tea-stain.

Liz cuts to the chase.

'How's your dad?' she asks me.

'All right. But not all right.'

'What do you mean?'

Bit by bit, I tell her. I describe the pub we went to, what I heard, the people I met, and my discovery that my dad's part of a group of right-wing bigots. It's such a relief to tell her all this. As I talk I feel my mind clearing, and even the light coming in through the windows seems brighter and more luminescent. Someone laughs in the distance. But Liz is listening to me in horror. That doesn't surprise me. It is pretty horrific. I also don't want my dad to be mixed up with this bunch.

Then she says something that does surprise me. 'I know all about this.'

Now I'm baffled. I wait for her to explain. She starts a story about her mum's boyfriend – that he's an undercover journalist – and that he was at the meeting last night. Immediately I know who he is – the short guy, the other new one.

'Shit,' I say. Which is pretty inadequate. So I add, 'What a coincidence!'

'Jimmy,' she says to me. 'You've got to get out.'

'Yeah, I know. But it isn't as easy as that.'

'Listen – this Fellowship of Albion. They instigate riots – they work alongside extreme right-wing groups – they're basically Neo-Nazis. They spread rumours – they get

211

involved in fights – they beat up Peter – I saw him, Jimmy – they'll stop at nothing. This is dangerous. You'll get hurt.'

'No,' I tell her. 'They're just a bunch of blokes in a pub talking big. You should have been there. The whole thing stinks, I know, and I'm going to talk to my dad and tell him I don't want to get involved.'

'Just get yourself out of there and out of his flat,' she says.

Now I feel myself getting angry. She's giving me orders. Here is this girl sitting in front of me and – here's the truth now – I fancy her – it's not something I can help – and maybe I always have – but she barges into my affairs and walks all over me and always knows best and . . .

She's crying.

Liz is crying. Large shimmering tears are welling up in her eyes. Her face is trembling.

'Liz?'

'I just don't want you to be involved in any of this,' she says. 'Just get out. You can go back home to your mum.'

She takes a serviette from the metal container on the table and blows her nose.

Blowing your nose isn't very romantic. In fact, I can't think of one movie where the heroine gets out a Kleenex and blasts out her nostrils. Not one. But as I'm sitting here I realise why Liz is crying – she doesn't have to tell me – she's crying because she cares what happens to me. She's scared for me. She's not telling me what to do at all. She just wants me to be OK.

This hits me like a whirlwind. All the months Liz and I

212

have been working together and trading insults – all the time I've been playing around with Sophie – all that time – we'd been drawing closer and closer together. Whether I like it or not, we're linked together. I can't explain it and I don't want to. Only I know that I feel closer to her now than to anyone else – Mum, Dad, whoever. While I've had my eyes shut, life has been organising this surprise for me.

For all her bluster, for all her tough girl act – inside Liz is as confused and scared as I am.

In the movie I'd reach across the table and kiss her now, even though her nose is red and her cheeks are damp. But something is stopping me.

This is what it is. I don't feel worthy of her. Here is gorgeous, clever, sorted Liz, who blew out her mates on results day to be with me, who wouldn't leave me alone with my dad as she didn't trust him, who was eaten up with jealousy while I messed around with Sophie – here she is, and what have I done for her? Nothing. Zero. Sod all.

My mum's words come back to me now. I have no sense of responsibility. I never think about the future. I spend all my time watching movies, hiding. That last thought is my own accusation at myself. I feel like I'm suddenly surfacing from a long sleep and it's morning. I'm wide awake. Liz has stopped crying now and sits there, sober and quiet.

'Look,' I say to her. 'It's not that easy. I can't just leave my dad without giving him a reason. So I'll have to have a showdown with him, and I'll have to pick my time carefully. If possible I don't want there to be hard feelings between us. He is my dad, after all.'

'He's your biological dad. But you've only known him for a few weeks.'

'Yeah, but I feel he's kind of dependent on me.'

As I say this, I realise it's absolutely true. I wonder whether all parents are like that – that they grow to need their own kids. For the right reasons, and for the wrong reasons.

'Jimmy – your dad is one of a bunch of racists. They're not just dangerous, but downright evil. They practise hatred. Your dad walked into your party and he saw Amir, he saw Amir's mates, he saw Charlene and JC – all of our people – and he hated them. So you choose, because you can't have both of them.'

She's crying again. She makes it sound very simple – your parents or your mates. Maybe growing up is about finding your true family – even making your own family.

I've made my choice.

'Liz – you'll have to let me sort this out myself. I need more time with my dad.'

'You're making a big mistake! Jimmy – please. Go back to the way you were. Don't get swallowed up by that .. man! Your dad isn't a good thing and you're just going to have to deal with that. And you – you're . . . you're the best person I know! Jimmy – I want you to be like you were!'

'I can't be,' I tell her, knowing that's the truth.

'Jimmy,' she says now, 'I could have loved you,' and she gets up, pushes her chair away, and it topples over, clattering on the wooden floor. Heads turn. Conversation stops. In a moment she's gone. And that's that.

LIZ'S DIARY

Monday, 27th August

Twelfth entry

It's over.

This is the epitaph: the inscription on the gravestone. I think I've wanted Jimmy secretly ever since I've known him. I fought my infatuation and I lost. All the time he was going out with Sophie I was jealous. Every time I wrote in this diary that I didn't care for him any more, I did. I was deluding myself.

But now it is finally over. I can't love someone who lets himself get swept into racism, or even sits quiet and says nothing. Because that's the same as allowing it to happen – there's no such thing as an innocent bystander. It didn't matter at all to me that Jimmy was a dreamer, that he fooled around, even that he doesn't quite know himself yet. Who does? But it matters to me that he won't stand up to his dad on this.

The way he wouldn't meet my eye in the art gallery café. The way he shifted nervously in his seat. The fact he said he needed more time with his dad. Even worse than loving someone who doesn't love you, is realising that the person you love is worthless. It's the worst kind of betrayal. I've betrayed myself.

I don't want to tell Maggie – I don't want anyone to know. I've never felt more alone in my life.

I don't know what to do.

JIMMY

I wonder if I've still got it in me to shoot a film. I can see how movies with their tidy ends and deliberate lies distort everything. They lead me away from dealing with the real issues. I've seen people in terms of their movie counterparts, and I've seen my whole life as some kind of Disney fantasy. Like my mum said, it's time to get real.

Summer's nearly ended, and luckily I've still got quite a bit of cash. I decide to go out and buy myself a parka – one with a big hood and wide, deep pockets. Grey or khaki. It'll come in useful for those cold mornings when I have to get up early for college.

In films, you always know what the ending is going to be. They give you clues – right from the beginning. Like in *Kill Bill* – Bill's gonna get killed, right? And in Richard Curtis movies everyone ends up getting married. You know it from the first scene in the airport lounge.

The difference with real life is that you have to trust to luck, to fate.

Do you know, it's more exciting *not* knowing what's going to happen.

*

I say to Dad, as we cut into our burgers, 'I enjoyed the meeting last night.'

'Did you?' He looks surprised, pleased. If a momentary doubt crosses his face it's soon replaced by unfeigned delight. His son was onside again. 'But you accused me of being racist!'

'Yeah. I know. But I've been thinking about what you said.' I stuffed some chips into my mouth, unconcerned. I chewed a while, swallowed. Should have put more vinegar on. Chips by themselves are just boring.

'This means a lot to me, Jimmy,' my dad says, serious.

I repeat, 'I know.' And carry on eating. One thing I'm learning already is how quickly you can make people believe something that they want to believe. My dad is already making plans for us.

'I could take you to another meeting. We're planning some action shortly – in Belton. I don't know how far you want to get involved . . .'

'Pretty far,' I say. 'There's no point in half measures.'

Maybe I was sounding too keen. My dad looks at me quizzically, his burger halfway to his mouth.

'Look – you're my dad,' I say. 'I trust you. You wouldn't get me into trouble.'

He smiles at me. 'You're right. And for that reason I don't want you getting involved in anything compromising. Just watch and learn.'

'I'd like that.'

'In fact,' he says, checking his watch, 'I could take you to a meeting tonight. We could get the car out of the garage and be there in fifteen minutes.'

I can't eat another mouthful. Chips and burger taste like mud. I swallow quickly and say, 'Let's go for it.'

Fate is definitely on my side. Not only is there a meeting tonight, but it's pouring with rain. So when I go to my room and get my new parka with its synthetic fur hood, Dad looks unsurprised. We throw the plates in the dishwasher and head out of the flat to the underground garage. I check the pocket of my parka. I get this slight sense of dissociation – like there's two Jimmys slightly out of sync with each other, one watching the other. Weird.

This time we don't drive all the way to Belton. We go in the direction of my home, Mum and Steve's place, and stop in the seedy part of town about a twenty-minute walk away. It's notorious, that part of town. A definite no-go area. There have been drug busts and a campaign to get rid of the street walkers. Every other kid's on an ASBO. We all avoid it on our way in or out of town. There are still old terraces of dirty red-brick houses with square, grimy windows, and bigger, older houses split into flats. Not all the street lights work. The paving stones are cracked.

We park in a cul-de-sac of red-brick semis and get out. I follow my dad up the garden path of one of them and wait while he rings at the bell. I check my pocket. It hits me that what I plan to do is dangerous, virtually impossible and downright crazy. Adrenaline is charging through me like wild horses.

The door opens and that Norman-guy ushers us in. He shakes my hand meaningfully. I think what an ugly bastard he is. Not on the outside – on the outside he's suave, clean-shaven, gleaming. But I know what lies beneath the surface and it makes me sick. Norman offers to take my parka and hangs it over the banister. I take a last, longing look at it and turn my attention to the layout of the house. It's just an everyday semi. There's a kitchen ahead of us and I notice there's a door leading to a back garden. We're taken into the room next to it, a compact living room with the usual furniture – again, nothing special. That's more frightening, in a way. That such ugly things can hide under a veil of normality. I want to capture that.

There are fewer people than at the last meeting. Just five of them and two of us. A few cans of lager are dotted around. I survey the room and my heart leaps when I see there's a hatch leading from the kitchen to the sitting room. Its two wooden shutters are ajar. There's a gap of about a couple of inches.

Now I'm not at all superstitious, but if I was, I'd say luck intended to be on my side tonight. So now I concentrate on seeming at ease. When I'm offered a lager I accept it very eagerly, and knock it back quickly. All part of the plan.

My dad is speaking about me. 'You can trust Jimmy,' he says. 'He's a good lad. I can vouch for him.'

Norman seems happy with that. Sometimes being a blood relation is a distinct advantage.

The lager tastes metallic and vile but I finish it and eye another. Someone indicates that it's fine to help myself. They all settle down to listen to Norman.

'Something very nasty indeed has come to my attention,' he says heavily. 'Something very nasty indeed. A white girl might have been sexually assaulted in Belton. But the police are covering it up – we think they don't want to upset things before the festival. It comes to a pretty poor pass when the English police are against the English people. It's like fighting a war out there.'

'Hear, hear,' says a bloke on an armchair by the fireplace. So ordinary-looking he could be a teacher or a bank clerk. I shudder.

Another takes up the tale – a bearded bloke with tiny, fierce black eyes. 'It's a war all right – and when the government come to us when Al-Qaida are roaming the streets killing Christians and ask us to defend our own, I'll remind them how they've made it impossible for us to own the guns we need to look after ourselves, and when Tony Blair comes begging—'

Norman speaks over him.

'So we've been doing our own investigations. This girl – your sister knows her, Martin – was taking a cab back from town, and the story goes she'd paid the driver and he argued that she hadn't given him enough, and he got into the back before she had a chance to get out. She was terrified. This Asian with a white cap perched on his head, twice her age, leering at her . . .'

''Scuse me,' I mumble. 'Need the bog.'

I've chosen my moment well. Everyone's engrossed with Norman's graphic account of the assault. I'm a quick worker. I put on my parka and steal into the kitchen. The sink is full of dirty plates. There's a stack of tabloid newspapers on the table. I position myself close to the wall where no one can see me through the hatch, and in a moment the camcorder's in my hand, my thumb switches it on and I'm praying that I'm at such an angle that no one spots me. I know not to risk this for longer than a moment or two.

But it's a good moment. Norman's voice gathers force and volume.

'So it's possible that he works for Star Plus cabs, his name could be Mr Aziz, and the registration number of his vehicle is ML03 BNF. Now I'm not saying he's the one, but—'

'I know some mates of mine who'd be interested in that,' says the bloke with the beard. 'Just in case he's also the bastard who mugged that old lady outside the post office.'

'I wouldn't put it past him. This Aziz is a young bloke. Fit. A moral degenerate.'

'Quite reasonable, then,' said my dad, 'if we express our feelings by doing something to his cab. At least we're not harming people, just property.'

Furious murmur of agreement at this. I catch the expression on the bearded guy's face – excited, fearful, his eyes glittering with cowardly mischief. I zoom in. What a shot! This is so cool. Everyone in the room is so intent on their plans the atmosphere is visibly electric. I'm picking all of this up. I pan out to the blank TV screen and the painting on the wall, then catch each man's face in turn.

Norman goes, 'I have a canister of petrol out there in the shed, and some other bits and pieces which might come in useful. But forget I said that. None of you would ever use them. You're all law-abiding citizens. Unlike the black scum who break the law on a daily basis. You'd never take action

222

without thinking this all through. You wouldn't want to spoil the Belton multicultural festival next week.'

There is a momentary pause, and my instinct tells me to cut and run. I move away from the gap in the hatch. I hesitate for just one moment. I could leave now, through the front door, but if there really is a shed out the back, with incriminating evidence . . .

I see there's a key in the back door. Very, very quietly, I turn it. I take a quick panoramic shot of the kitchen as a visual farewell – I use the image of the filthy crockery in the sink to symbolise my directorial disgust – and slip out into the back yard. There's the shed. It's locked. Not sure what to do now. The rain is still coming down and I hide the camcorder under my parka. That's when I see a tiny crack in the wood. Glad that I've already investigated where the night vision button on the camcorder is situated, I stand on tiptoes and point my silver machine inside. On the screen I see a drum and by it, on the floor, what look like some coshes.

Then I hear my dad call, 'Jimmy?'

I'm almost about to go back in the house when I wonder how I'm going to explain being out here in the pouring rain when I should have gone upstairs. I shove the camcorder back in my pocket and notice there's a gate at the end of the yard. Praying it isn't locked I make towards it, undo the bolt, and I'm out into a back alley with brick walls on either side. As I run off, I hear loud and vicious barking. There's the sound of something being unchained.

Fear gives me wings. I'm out of the alley and into a street

I don't recognise. Some kids in hoodies hanging about under a lamp post eye me with interest. The barking is getting louder. I shoot off, trying to get as far away from the alley as I can, the camcorder banging against my leg as I run. My chest is tight and my lungs hurt. I turn the corner into another, long road, and really don't have a clue where I am. But I feel fairly certain I've shaken off my dad.

I carry on running, but my legs feel like marshmallow and I can tell I'm slowing. I veer between crazy joy at the idea I might have pulled it off, and fear that I might hear a car behind me and discover I'm being pursued.

There's someone coming towards me, running. A sturdily-built man. I don't know whether to turn and run back the way I came. I begin to understand what I've just done, and what might happen if I'm caught. The man is catching up on me, but as he gets nearer I find I don't recognise his face. As he passes me I call to him to tell me where the main road is. He answers by pointing behind him.

And here I am, on the main road, the road I know well – the road that will take me straight to my old home – my real home. I slow down. I'm walking now as the night sets in and the rain comes down, one foot in front of the other along this familiar road. I'm ignoring the waves of nausea in my stomach and the way my mind flashes back to where my dad – to where Mike is now – what he's thinking and doing. Past the salon where my mum used to work, past the vet's, along by the garage where a welcoming light comes from the paying booth. Over the crossroads, and I soon turn into my street. Here I am.

Here's my house. There's the wheelie bin with the number 32 painted on it by Steve. There's Mum and Steve in the front room. They haven't closed the curtains yet. I walk up the garden path and unlock the door.

I call out, 'I'm home!'

Mum meets me in the corridor. She takes in my bedraggled appearance and I see her trying to make sense of it.

'Is this is a visit?' she asks. 'Or are you . . .'

'Back for good.' I complete her sentence. 'I'm back for good.'

'Well, get that parka off,' she says. 'You're dripping all over the carpet.'

I'm glad she tells me off. I don't feel I can deal with all the emotion slushing around me. My mum and I have never done the sloppy stuff. Maybe her carping has been a substitute for that. In a flash I understand that a lone woman bringing up a boy might feel it's better to be tough and to set boundaries. To keep her distance. I'm standing here looking at her with my new clear vision and seeing things from her point of view. All those years worrying that I might turn out like my dad. In the beginning not having anyone to help her make decisions about me. But now I feel something spark between us and know – perhaps I've always known – that we are connected, and always will be. That's what it means to love a parent. You don't always agree with them, and sometimes you can't stand them. But there they are – there they'll always be.

I don't say any of this. I'm not even sure those words are formulated in my head. I thank her silently for not making a fuss. I thank Steve for not coming out and leaving us alone together.

I tell her I'd like go up to my room for a bit. She says that's OK with her, and I lope up the stairs and it's good to be home, really good. The old place has a smell all of its own, a multicoloured swirl of carpet and damp, of Mum's perfume and dust, of crayons and kids.

My room's missed me. The bed is clean and tidy, duvet straight and tight over the sheet, it's the navy and white striped cover. There's no mess anywhere. So I open my wardrobe and fling a few things around, just to make me feel at home. I wonder how it must have been for Mum, to come up and here and tidy up after me, thinking I might have left for good. I feel ashamed – but also embarrassed – the thought of my mum picking up gear that hadn't seen the inside of the washing machine for months.

I hang the parka on the hook on the back of door and get the camcorder out. I sit at my desk and play back the tape I shot. On a tiny screen, no bigger than a credit card, I watch and listen to the Albion blokes construct their plot. I've held the camera steady, and the picture quality is good. I like the way I focus on each one in turn and zoom in – the composition of the shot is good, too. I can see how – when I edit this on my computer – I can lose a few dead moments and tighten the whole thing up. Now there's a pause, and the action moves to the shed – it's dark, but the machine adjusts and – yes – you can see the petrol, and the coshes – and then the commotion as Dad calls my name – and it all goes black and fuzzy. Success! Unbelievable.

Of course, there's going to be a problem if I want to edit it properly. I left the computer software at Park Point. And if anyone wanted to play the film back, they'd need the correct software. That shouldn't be a problem, though. Not if . . . not if . . .

Now, for the first time, I ask myself what I was doing, shooting all of this. The simple answer is that I did it for Liz. There was no other way I could make her believe that I wasn't on board with my dad, and that I had the courage to blow the whistle on him. I wanted to impress her – I wanted to present her with the solid evidence that I had guts.

So, OK, I've done it. Now what? I give the tape to Liz. And she will pass it on to her mum's bloke. And he will show it to his editor, and his editor will contact the police. And they'll track down Norman and the bearded guy and all the rest of them and get them for incitement to racial hatred – along with my dad.

Along with my dad. Unbelievably, this hasn't hit me till now. But if I hand over this tape, my dad could face jail.

Carefully I place the camcorder down on my desk. It was a present from my dad, and I've used it to get him arrested. I'm feeling slightly sick now – a chill pricks at my skin. I didn't mean that to happen. I just wanted to impress Liz. So, fine. I can destroy the tape, give Dad back the camcorder, tell him I think I'll stay at Mum's for a while. But if I do that, and the day before the Belton festival someone sets fire to a minicab, and there's a riot, whose fault will it be?

Answer – the person who didn't let the authorities know what was being planned.

Now I get this mad idea I can make an anonymous call to the press or the police with my information. But if I do that there's still a good chance my dad will end up being questioned, and he'll work out that I could easily have been involved. And if I choose that route, I'll also know that I've turned yellow. It's a cowardly compromise. Like Liz said, it's all about choices. Either I shop my dad, or play along with the racists.

Mike is my dad – but I've only known him for a month or so. That ought to make it easier, but in some way I don't understand, it makes it worse. He comes into my life, showers me with worldly goods and uncritical affection, and what do I do? Get him arrested.

What do I owe him? He helped form me and brought me into this world. He's as much a part of me as my mum is. He's misguided, dangerous and altogether a nasty piece of work. I don't have to be like him and I don't want to be; I know now I want to have as little to do with him as possible. But get him into serious trouble? I don't think so.

I play for time by taking the tiny tape out of the machine. I open a drawer of my desk and place it in one corner. It sits there snug and neat, innocent-looking. Yeah, right. It's incriminating evidence. If I hand it over, my dad will know it was me who caught him in the act, me who betrayed him. Can I live with that?

My thoughts are chasing each other's tails. I can't reach a decision. For all my nerve in taking this damn film, I don't know if I've got what it takes to use it. I don't even know what I *should* do. I wish someone would tell me what to do. I need advice. I need my mum.

I walk to the door and turn off the light. I make my way downstairs where a light is glowing and the television murmurs soothingly. This is something I can't do alone.

LIZ'S DIARY

Tuesday 28th August

Thirteenth entry

I'm going to record all of this exactly as it happened. Starting yesterday.

Late yesterday night, Peter came round. He looked drawn and distant. I knew immediately something bad had happened and Maggie did too. But neither of us are very used to dealing with men and their emotions. We weren't sure whether to ask him what was wrong, or just tread carefully around him. His brow was furrowed and his movements awkward. There was some small talk, but it trickled away. That was when it occurred to me that maybe he wanted to speak to Maggie alone. The flash of irritation I had that we were both competing for her attention died very quickly, as I sensed his problems might be greater than mine. So I pretended I had something to do upstairs and Maggie threw me a grateful look.

They must have been talking for an hour or so. At least, it was about an hour later when Maggie called me down. Peter had gone. She looked hollow and empty. For one moment I wondered whether he'd split with her, and the thought sent me into a panic. Had I brought this on? Was it my stupid behaviour? Maggie attempted a brave smile.

'Not good news, I'm afraid. It looks like Peter's being transferred to London.'

'Why?'

'Vince Cooper's been able to make a case for closing the northern office of the paper. The editor's thinking it over. And if he decides to go ahead, Peter's got no option but to leave the city, unless he fancies being unemployed for a while.'

'Can't he go freelance?'

'It's not that easy to make a living like that.'

I could feel Maggie's aching disappointment in my body. What made it so much worse is that I'd hoped for this – hoped that something would happen that would stop us two becoming three. It was almost as if the strength of my wishes had created this reality – I'd made it happen. I hated this power I seemed to have. I never meant to make Maggie miserable. Instead I said, 'It's because the riot investigation failed, isn't it?'

'Basically, yes. If Peter had pulled that off, he'd have been the hero of the hour. There would have been no way they could have afforded to get rid of him. The story would have been huge.'

'What will you do?' I asked her.

'We'll manage,' she said. 'There'll be weekends. Come here.'

I did, and she hugged me tight. As I tried to answer the pressure of her hug and send my love out to her, still an evil voice whispered to me, *you wanted this to happen, you* made *this happen.* I was being irrational, because I had done nothing but wish. Yet I felt as guilty as if I'd engineered the whole thing.

Maggie put a brave face on it. 'Who knows what might turn up?' she said. 'And if two people want to be together, nothing can really stop them.' I agreed with her, and we stayed up late to watch a film. I didn't sleep much that night, and neither did she, I guess.

Disappointment and misery aren't just abstract, I was learning. You can taste their sourness and feel it inside you. It drags at you and weighs down your limbs. It robs you of all of your energy. At least Bob put my bad mood down to the fact me and Jimmy had failed to become a happy couple. He laid off me, and I went around work the next day like an automaton. Luckily Jimmy wasn't on my shift. It was me, Bob, Charlene, and a new person they'd sent up – a Chinese student who was a quick learner.

The good thing about work is that it takes your mind off things. Correction; it takes your mind off things temporarily, because every so often it broke into my head like a newsflash – Peter's off to London and your evil fairy wishes have come true. Worse than that, the absence of Jimmy, and the absence of my dreams about Jimmy, were a black hole inside me. I couldn't get used to not wanting him.

You think you're in control of your life, but you're not. Not ever.

There was a rush on. I was at the bar. I was spooning milk into cappuccinos, and placing the drinks on the serving point, where they were being carried off by impatient customers. There was a gaggle of them waiting for their drinks, some of them even uncertain what they had ordered. Finally I put down the last espresso. I turned to get some paper roll to wipe the bar where there were spots of milk. I wiped the bar, threw the paper in the bin behind me, turned again, and standing at the serving point was Jimmy.

My stomach lurched and I wanted to cry. I realised you can't stop loving someone just like that. But as glad as I was to see him, the knowledge that he'd turned out so weak made the pain I was feeling worse. I stood there and didn't know what to do.

'Have you got a break coming up?' he asked.

I did.

'I'll wait for you,' he said, and went and sat by the window.

I didn't see how a replay of yesterday's conversation would benefit either of us. I decided I wouldn't go over and join him. But as the minutes ticked away, I felt my resolve weaken. I would speak to him, if only to spell out that there was no possibility of us ever being a couple. Not now.

I was all fingers and thumbs. I had to concentrate hard on what I was doing. But eventually the time came when I was free to go and join Jimmy. I went to sit down by him but he said, 'Not here,' and I followed him out of the shop. We came to a halt outside a little church – funny how I'd never really noticed it was there before. Jimmy said, 'I have a present for you.'

What? Was he trying to win me over with a pathetic gift of

chocolates or flowers? I could hardly believe it. He reached into his pocket and gave me an envelope. Puzzled, I asked if I should open it. He told me to go ahead.

Inside was a miniature tape. I asked him what it was.

'You'll need to get hold of the right software,' he said. 'For a Sony camcorder – I've made a note of the details and it's in the envelope too. I shot the film last night.'

I was all at sea. In the middle of the big mess he's in, Jimmy finds the time to make a movie!

'I went with my dad to another meeting. It's all on the tape. What they plan to do, where they meet, everything.'

It took some time for this to sink in. Stupidly I repeated everything he told me. 'You mean you went with your dad and shot a film of him and his cronies? Did he know you were doing this?'

Jimmy shook his head.

'So you were *spying* on them?'

No response. Meaning that he was. My brain was slowly assimilating all of this. He'd taped what they were up to. He wasn't really on his dad's side at all. In fact he'd gone under-cover without even telling me.

'I thought your mum's bloke might be interested,' he muttered, diffidently.

A man in a dog collar came out of the church and smiled at us. I kind of smiled back. Three women swished passed us with designer carrier bags. We were the still centre in the bustling city street.

For the second time I repeated everything to him, to

be certain I was getting it right. 'So this is a tape of that Fellowship and you're giving it to Peter so he can blow the whistle on them?'

'Yep,' he said.

I shoved to the back of my mind what this would mean for Peter, although I knew I would have to get this to him as quickly as possible. Because the enormity of what Jimmy had chosen hit me and almost winded me.

'Is your dad on this tape?'

'Mmm.'

'He'll get into trouble, won't he?'

'Yeah.' Then Jimmy found his voice.

'Liz – I didn't know what to do. I shot the film because of – well, let's just say I shot it anyway. And then I spoke to my mum – I'm living there again now.' Jimmy's phone announced a message. He checked it. 'My dad. He's texting or ringing every ten minutes or so.' He switched the phone off. 'He doesn't know where I am. I didn't go back to the flat last night.'

I sat down on the steps of the church. Jimmy joined me. We didn't touch.

'I spoke to my mum,' he said again. 'I didn't know what to do – whether to hand my dad over or let him go free. This is how she saw it. With her being my mum and everything, she kind of puts me first.'

'Parents do that,' I added.

'She reckoned if, knowing what I know, I said nothing and it was found out I was at two meetings of the Fellowship,

235

I could get into trouble too. She said they were breaking the law, and how could I prove I wasn't in with them? But that wasn't what decided me.'

'What did?'

'Well, just say I destroyed the tape and said nothing. And then there was a riot. And someone got killed. Then I'd sort of be responsible. That person could be someone's mum or dad. Or son or daughter. So the choice was between getting my dad arrested, or risking someone else's dad getting killed. When Mum put it like that . . .'

What could I say? Then he went on:

'She also said I should tell him what I've done. She said I owed it to him. She said it was cowardly just to walk out of his life, then do this. I've got to explain myself.'

'Have you?'

'Not yet.'

'Oh, OK.'

We sat there in silence for – how long? – one minute? Two minutes? It was a long time, anyway. Then he reached over and held my hand. I squeezed his hand. It was enough. Just sitting there holding hands. Holding hands so tightly I knew we were never going to let go. Tears pricked at my eyes.

He said, 'I did this for you.'

I said, 'I know. And it worked. You've got me.'

The pressure of his hand increased. My eyes filled with tears now.

I sniffed, and said, 'I think we'd better get the tape to Peter.'

We stood up, and that was when we kissed. Right there in

the middle of the street. Clinging together. Not caring what anyone else thought. Me and Jimmy.

But it was me who broke away first. 'The tape,' I said. I got my phone out, rang the store, told Bob I might be late back. He said not to worry as business had dropped.

Together Jimmy and I walked quickly to the newspaper office. We pushed through the swing doors, went straight up to the receptionist behind the desk and asked to see Peter Taylor. She asked who we were. It seemed ages before she could track him down and finally he came to us from out of the lift.

He looked surprised to see me. I explained very quickly what we had and he grasped the implications immediately. Jimmy explained about the software and Peter said, did we mind if he took the tape and played it back as soon as possible. We said that was fine and I left my mobile number with him, so he could update us on what was happening.

He said to Jimmy, 'You're a hero.' He said nothing to me, but the way he smiled at me meant he didn't need to.

In a few moments we were back out on the street. Jimmy said to me that I'd better get back to work and we'd meet up later. Now he had to see his dad.

I got out my phone and rang Bob again. 'Bob,' I said. 'Look – I'm not feeling too good. I'm going to have to take the rest of the afternoon off. Women's troubles!' I announced triumphantly. I've noticed that men never ask you for details when you say that. Even gay men.

I turned to Jimmy. 'I'm coming with you,' I said.

'I can cope with him,' he told me, taking my hand again.

'I don't doubt it for one moment,' I said. 'But I'm not letting you go now.'

We kissed again, just briefly. It felt wrong to be so happy in the midst of this awful drama. But I was – we were – and that's a fact. Then Jimmy switched his phone on and there were a queue of messages from his dad. This time he rang back. He told his dad he was coming round now.

It was a fifteen-minute walk to Park Point. On the way I explained to Jimmy about Peter's threatened relocation. I told him how this tape might change everything.

'He'll be able to stay in the city, and be with Maggie. He'll be able to renew the lease on his flat.'

'Is that good?'

'Not exactly. Because I'd pretty much made up my mind I don't mind him moving in with us.'

'Makes sense,' said Jimmy, 'if they're really into each other.'

'Perfect sense,' I said. And I meant it.

Jimmy and I had our first argument outside Park Point. I wanted to go in with him but he said he had to be alone with his dad. I said, what if his father got violent? He said that would never happen. I wasn't so sure.

Opposite Park Point is a little garden with beds of tired-looking flowers and a few pigeons strutting around. That was where I decided to wait. It was from there I watched Jimmy disappear and the metal doors close behind him.

JIMMY

The warm afterglow of Liz lingers with me as I climb the stairs and come out in the atrium. But the sight of the barren internal garden sobers me and I take a deep breath. So, OK, I know this isn't going to be easy. And to help myself I've prepared a speech. I've rehearsed it in my head over and again. My mum approves of it. All I have to do is walk in, deliver it, and go. That's all I have to do.

I don't use my key but rap at the door. That's symbolic, sort of. I don't live here any more. Dad's there in an instant, his face a mixture of terror and relief. He gets me inside and closes the door. I follow him into the living room. I'm surprised to see it's in disarray. Normally my dad keeps everything in military precision. But now books and clothes litter the place; there are unwashed cups and plates on the coffee table. I don't have time to notice anything else. Because he starts shouting at me. I'm terrified – I'm out of my depth here – I don't know this man at all, I don't know what he's going to do next.

'What the hell do you mean, running out on me like that? How do you think I felt, in front of my comrades? If you didn't like what you heard, then you had no right to go with me. It was your idea, remember. And where's your camcorder? Why didn't you come home last night? Or answer my calls? Now listen, my lad, if you're going to go on living here with me, as my son, you've got to learn discipline. You're going to learn to be reliable. Discipline is what you need. You'll obey orders. Behaviour like last night's is not going to be repeated. Do you hear me? Say something. Tell me you've heard this.'

His voice fills the room like a barrage of gunfire. I realise I've never heard him lose his temper up till now.

'Give me a chance,' I say to him, sounding weedy and pathetic.

'I don't want to hear your excuses, son. I want guarantees that I can rely on you in the future. And I want an apology.'

'I'm sorry,' I say, as much to stop him as anything else. But I am sorry. It's the truth.

Up to that moment he's been towering over me, rigid with something that looked very much like hatred. But he stops shouting now, he's breathing heavily, and then calms down. He likes my apology. He thinks he's won. He can't hide his triumph. He wants to consolidate his victory.

'OK,' he says. 'I think we'll have to establish some ground rules from this point.'

'Dad,' I cut in. 'Can I say something?'

'Sometimes things have to done that don't sound that pretty, Jimmy. One day you'll understand this. Young people are idealistic. I know that. Even Colin took issue with me on occasion. But he would have come round, and you will too. I can show you some things—'

'Dad,' I try again. 'I do have something to say.'

240

'The floor's yours,' he tells me. The switch from ogre to relaxed dad terrifies me. I'm beginning to realise just how unpredictable and changeable Mike is. But I summon my resolve. Hell. I can't remember anything I planned to say to him. Not that it matters. My mouth is so dry no words will come out anyway. But he's waiting now, curious, looking at me as a cat does a mouse that he knows he can decimate with one bat of his paw.

'I just want to tell you,' I say, in a small voice that sounds nothing like me, 'that I've decided to go back to Mum. I don't think it's working out, us living together. We'll stay in touch and everything. And I'm very grateful for everything you've done for me.'

Dad is smiling and shaking his head. It's not that he's disagreeing with me – he's denying me permission to go. He's not going to let me. So I summon all my resolve. I recall the words I was going to use. I face him across the space of the living room. The city street is our backdrop. I can't see Liz as she's at the other side of the building.

'I'm going to give you back the camcorder,' I said. 'I left it at Mum's. The fact is, I took it with me last night. I wanted to make a film of you. You know I'm interested in film, right? And I've got to start somewhere. And it came out quite well. But I realised I couldn't keep it to myself – because you were all breaking the law. And so I gave the tape to a journalist – and he—'

I was talking at breakneck speed. Dad has turned white, and I can see veins protruding in his forehead, near his scars.

'You what?' he whispers. 'You gave that film to a journalist?'

'Yeah. I'm sorry. But in the end I had no choice. I—'

I don't see it coming. I can't duck to avoid it. My dad's fist smashes into my face. Something warm and sticky's trickling from my nose. There's no pain that I'm aware of. Well, there might be, but it was somewhere else in the room. I put my hand to my nose to stem the flow of blood. In a way I'm glad he hit me. Maybe I deserve it.

Next thing I know, he's got me on the floor. He's crouching over me. I can feel his hot breath on my face. His face is distorted with rage and grief. His spit hits my face as he talks.

'You bastard,' he says. 'You're no son of mine. I knew it from the beginning. Your mother's a whore. You aren't my son.'

I'm thinking, will he kill me?

'You betrayed me,' he says. Sweat glistens on his bulging forehead.

I turn my face away from him. I don't want to see what will happen next.

He slaps my face hard. I wince with the sharp, acid pain. He's shouting and cursing me. He's got me pinned me down, I'm completely overpowered by him. Now his fingers are around my neck, squeezing at my throat. If I don't fight back, he'll kill me. This is not a joke, this is really happening. I start kicking him but the pressure of his fingers only tightens. Then from my pocket my mobile starts ringing. My ringtone is from *Saturday Night Fever* – 'Stayin' Alive'.

We both stop and listen. It's not quite the movie

242

soundtrack I'd imagined for my big moment, but it does the trick.

My dad takes his fingers from my throat. His concentration on me slackens. I can see a new thought has hit him. The tone plays on. Eventually it stops. I guess someone is leaving a message. Not John Travolta.

Dad lumbers up and stands above me.

'Get up,' he mutters. 'And count yourself lucky.'

I'm in a sitting position now. There's blood on the carpet. Mine.

My dad asks me, very deliberately, 'When did you pass the tape over?'

'About half an hour ago.'

'Half an hour. OK. I've got to pop out for a while. I have to see to some things. I want you to stay here. Because if you don't, I really am going to have to . . .'

But he doesn't finish his sentence. He's searching his pockets for his keys. I watch him take his jacket, glance around him, and take one final look at me. In his eyes I'm reflected back as something poisonous and vile. I've been disowned. I watch him leave the flat. The door slams. He's gone. I find I'm listening for the sound of a bolt being fitted but there's nothing. Just emptiness.

I don't get up immediately – I don't think I have the strength. And slowly it dawns on me what my dad is doing. He's saving his own skin. He's doing a runner. Maybe he's warning his mates – and maybe he isn't. So he won't face the music, and in a way, I'm not surprised. I'm sickened by his selfishness, but also pleased that he might escape. Because he is my dad after all, though he's a nasty piece of work.

And here I am alone in this apartment, and I know it's going to be for the last time. I could almost pretend now that this *is* my apartment. Only I don't want to. The apartment is unreal, like a movie set. The only real thing here is me. Sitting here with a bloodied nose. It hurts like hell. I'm dazed and not able to get up and walk out of here, not yet.

When I do, I'm going to have to begin all over again. I'll have to learn how to walk again.

I know the blow to my nose has left me light-headed. I ought to do whatever it is you do for shock, have a cup of sweet tea or something. Whatever. But now I think I'm ready to get out of here.

So I do. I stagger up and look around me for the last time. I remember Mike's command that I should stay put, and his threat, but I discount it almost immediately. I realise that he was scared – more scared than me – and once I walk out of here, there's nothing he can do to me. I also know he'd never take revenge – in his own way, he loves me. Weird but true. And if he turns up again, that's what I'll have to deal with. His love, not his hatred.

I leave the flat, double-lock the door, walk through the atrium and down the steps. That's it. The end of the movie where Jimmy meets his real dad. And loses him. But this is where real life starts.

As I leave Park Point I look for Liz. And there she is. I stumble towards her. I'm a bit confused by the look of horror on her face, but then acknowledge that I am covered in blood.

She's dabbing at me with tissues, asking me what hurts, and what happened, and I like this feeling of being looked after, taken care of. I tell her bit by bit what my dad did.

'It's lucky I rang you,' she comments dryly.

I kind of knew it was her.

Me and Liz. This is reality. I'm beginning to see that reality can be better than the movies. There's still stuff I have to pick up, I know. I owe my mum an apology too. And I need to get back to college. Now life's done the worst it can to me, I'm no longer scared . . .

What the hell am I on about?

I ask Liz if she doesn't mind being bled all over while I kiss her.

She says, 'What is this, something out of Tarantino?'

'No,' I say, 'It's for real.'

LIZ'S DIARY

Sunday 9th September

Final entry

I've not written in my diary for ages – too busy. But Jimmy's gone now and Maggie and Peter are still at the Belton festival. It was great. Charlene and Amir were there too – we were dancing in the street. Then Jimmy and I came back here early. Then – you don't expect me to put *everything* in my diary . . .

We start back at college tomorrow, and things couldn't be more different to what they were back in July. Jimmy is going to a different college, a place where he can study film, unlike the college he went to where he was doing the wrong courses. That's partly why it didn't work for him last year. I'm certain of it.

I've met his mum. She is really nice! I didn't realise she did manicures too and she said if I come round one evening she'll do my nails with any design I want on them. How cool is that? She reminds me loads of Jimmy – she looks like him – I mean he looks like her – and the kids are great. His little brother is so cute!

I'm rambling. All these new people in my life. And just to

put it in writing, Peter's moving in. Once the Fellowship of Albion story broke, everything changed at the paper. There were meetings, new decisions. His job was saved. It was that evil Vince Cooper who was transferred to London. Good riddance! Sometimes there are fairy-tale endings!

After we found that out, I had a heart-to-heart with Maggie. I told her it made sense if Peter moved in. She was very emotional about it, but I was OK. I knew I'd given Peter my mum the moment I gave him that tape. That was my intention, and it came off.

And I haven't even recorded what happened to Mike. He did a runner – a complete runner. The police were able to round up a couple of the guys but Mike has vanished. He's not been in touch with Jimmy – it's like he's disappeared off the face of the earth. Jimmy's been worried whether he's OK, but his mum reckons he doesn't have the guts to harm himself, and she should know.

That camcorder – Jimmy couldn't give it back as his dad had gone, so we all decided to take it back to the store. We donated the money they gave us to a drop-in centre in Belton that gives advice to immigrants. That felt good.

And then – this is amazing – Peter and Maggie clubbed together – get this – without telling *me* – and bought him a new one – a new camcorder. He took it with him today and shot a movie of the festival. That's why he went early – he wants to edit it and later he's going to e-mail it to me.

He brought the camcorder round here after the festival, and left it downstairs . . .

I should think so too!